Acclaim for the Nick Polo Mystery Series

"A California PI himself, Kenneally captures some of the classic Hammett/Ross spirit in the Nick Polo series."

—*Publishers Weekly*

"Briskly written, and because Kennealy himself was a working private eye, most persuasive."

—*Philadelphia Inquirer*

"The Polo series all have a strong tradition of tight plotting, crisp dialogue, and self-deprecating humor."

—*Booklist*

"Kennealy writes crisply, brings alive the streets of San Francis-co, and plots clearly and interestingly."

—*Washington Post*

"The writing is simple and direct, the action nonstop."

—*The New York Times*

I'M DYING AS FAST AS I CAN

ALSO BY JERRY KENNEALY

Nick Polo Mystery Series
Polo Solo
Polo, Anyone?
Polo's Ponies
Polo in the Rough
Polo's Wild Card
Green with Envy
Special Delivery
Vintage Polo
Beggar's Choice
All That Glitters
Polo's Long Shot

Johnny O'Rorke Series
Screen Test
Dirty Who?

Carroll Quint Series
Jigsaw
Still Shot

Stand Alones
Nobody Wins
The Conductor
The Forger
The Suspect
The Hunted
The Other Eye
Cash Out
The Vatican Connection
Chasing the Devil
Silent Remains

JERRY KENNEALY

I'M DYING AS FAST AS I CAN

A Nick Polo Mystery

Down & Out Books
3959 Van Dyke Road, Suite 265
Lutz, FL 33558
DownAndOutBooks.com

Cover design by JT Lindroos

ISBN: 1-64396-080-6
ISBN-13: 978-1-64396-080-7

For my two beautiful daughters-in-law,
Patty and Maria

CHAPTER 1

"I'm dying as fast as I can," Gabriela Maoret said. "That's what I've been telling them. At first it was kind of a joke and got a laugh, but not anymore."

Gabriella was five-four or so, slim, and had the upright posture that comes from a lifetime of yoga or disciplined exercising. She had a face that cried out for a black-and-white photo portrait by Mark Coggins or Richard Avedon, weathered by too much sun, with too many laugh and frown lines, but full of life. The color of her eyes shifted somewhere between gray and green and still had a twinkle when she set her mind to it. Her nose was narrow, her mouth full, her shiny white hair hung straight down and ended with an inward curl below her chin. Her raspy voice signaled an affection for cigarettes.

She was wearing creased denim slacks, a black silk turtleneck and gray corduroy slippers that curled up at the toe.

She looked familiar, and I was searching my mind to try to remember just where I'd seen her before.

We were sitting in the living room of a three-story stucco-front early Art Moderne house that had been built in the 1930s at the dead end, that was before the Realtors started calling them cul-de-sacs, of the steep incline on Greenwich Street, in the posh Telegraph Hill area of San Francisco. It was a fully detached home, rare in most parts of San Francisco. The east side of the property butted up against Pioneer Park, five acres of pine and cypress trees that surrounded the circular drive leading up to the famed Coit Tower.

It was a large room furnished with low, comfortable chairs and couches upholstered in warm autumn colors.

The ceiling was latte colored. There was no way to tell the color of the walls—every inch of space was covered with paintings in a variety of styles or framed photographs of people hunting, fishing, swimming, playing tennis or golf, at a racetrack or just staring pleasantly at the camera lens.

To the left was an open arched wall showing a small dining room with a walnut table and five Danish modern chairs.

She tapped the ashes from an unfiltered Lucky Strike into an ashtray shaped like a violin and said, "Call me Gaby, everyone does. What do I call you? Mr. Polo?"

"Nick works fine. But why did you call me, Gaby?"

"Jimmy Feveral suggested I contact you. He thought you could help me."

She ground out her cigarette in the ashtray and smiled. "It's all Jimmy's fault, anyway. He's the one who wrote up the lifetime estate agreement years ago, so that I could live in this beautiful house until I kick the bucket."

James Feveral was a topnotch attorney and one of my best clients. He'd sent me an email with Gabriella's address and phone number, but without any background information, just a short note: "Good luck. You may need it."

Jim had taken off for a three-week vacation in Paris, to meet with his daughter Laura. Laura and I had a "relationship" but she had scooted off to Paris over a month ago to study art in Montmartre. I was beginning to get the feeling that she might have become more interested in the artists than their paintings.

Gaby lit up another Lucky, blew a smoke ring and put her index finger through it. "I'm going to be *sev-en-ty five* years old next month," she said with an exaggerated stutter. "I remember going to friends' birthdays when they turned seventy and feeling sorry for them. Old age."

"They say that seventy-five is the new fifty, Gaby."

"Yeah, and that nine-thirty is the new midnight. Let me put you in the picture. This house belonged to Gaucho Carmichael. Have you heard of him?"

"No. Should I have?"

"He was a character," she said. "Ethan Carmichael. His father, Ian, was Scottish, his mother Argentinian. He was born in Argentina. They moved to Texas when Ethan was nine or ten. He quickly adopted the 'Gaucho' name. It gave him some color, made him stand out from the crowd, and he loved that."

The Lucky got a deep inhale before she continued. "His mother died young. She'd had some money, her family owned a cattle ranch near Entre Rios, on the pampas, but his father went through that in a hurry. He was an oil wildcatter and a gambler, a bad one. Lost everything they had. He dug his own grave in the backyard, laid down and shot himself in the head. I guess he didn't want to make a mess.

"So Gaucho took over the family, which consisted of his two younger brothers, Logan and Niven. And he did well. Oil, at first, then he branched out. Radio stations, real estate and construction, flipping homes and commercial properties. He made a fortune.

"When we met it was lust at first sight. There was lots of sex, lots of drinking, lots of fighting, lots of makeup sex and more fighting. We traveled everywhere. All over Europe, Africa, and the Far East. He was going through an Ernest Hemingway stage of his life: fishing, hunting, racetracks. We'd be together for a while, then break up, and get back together."

Gaby pushed herself to her feet and crooked a finger at me. "Take a look."

She pointed out a photograph on the wall. "That's us after a run with the bulls in Pamplona, Spain."

A younger version of Gaby was leering at the camera, her arm wrapped around the waist of a broad-shouldered man with a black mustache similar in size and shape to the one Kevin Branagh wore in the latest version of *Murder on the Orient Express*. They were both dressed in traditional bull-running attire: white pants and shirts, red scarfs and waistbands, as well as black berets.

"Gaucho said I saved his life that day. He'd gotten too close to the bulls and I yanked him into a doorway." Her finger tapped a nearby photo. "Here we are in Africa, after a hunt."

It was a campfire scene. A good-sized animal was being roasted on a spit. Both Gaucho and Gaby held drinks in their hands. He was bare-chested and wearing a pair of those pleated Gurka shorts that Hemingway favored. His hair was dark, thick and curly.

"That's an impala on the spit. Gaucho liked playing the big white hunter. He owned all kinds of guns: rifles, shotguns, pistols. He loved the shooting part, but left all of the dressing and butchering to me. I made sure he only shot animals we could eat and give to the natives. If he wanted lions or giraffes he had to shoot them with his Leica."

The photo tour continued through India, Paris, South Africa and the Bahamas, the two of them standing on a fishing pier alongside a huge marlin hanging from a rope. They both aged gracefully, Gaby never seeming to put on a pound; Gaucho's hair turning gray, but his monster of a mustache remaining black.

"You two seemed to have good times together," I said.

"We had great times. We started living together off and on when I was forty-one, eight years older than Gaucho. It wasn't a big deal at first, but as time passed, it started to matter."

"You never married?"

"No. We both thought that would have ruined the relationship, and I think we were right. Gaucho had two marriages, and both of them were disasters."

I pointed to one of the paintings on the wall, a muted abstract of gold and blue. "I like this one."

"Thanks. It's one of mine." She waved a hand in the air. "All of them are. I taught for years at the San Francisco Art Institute. That's one of the things Gaucho admired about me. I gave him a real education on the art world. He wasn't interested in the paintings themselves, he purchased them as investments."

She closed her eyes and sighed. "God, I led him to some wonderful Picassos, a Monet, a few by Degas and Coubet, as well as some great abstract artists like Rothko and Kline, before they became so disgustingly expensive. He'd hold on to them for a few years and then put them up for auction. 'Better than real estate, and you don't have to put up with labor unions or crazy tenants,' he liked to say."

Another of the photos caught my attention—two young girls in modest one-piece swimsuits on a sunny beach.

"Is that you?"

"Yes, me and my sister Ava, on the beach in Sanremo, Italy. She's still there."

"You look like twins."

"No, I'm eleven months older than Ava."

"You're both beautiful. Give me a little background, Gaby. Are you married?"

"No. Never have been."

"Children?"

"No. Infertility. That's one of the reasons I never married. What was the sense of it? But Ava made up for me. She's a real old-fashioned Italian mama. Six kids. Four girls, two boys."

She ground out the half-smoked cigarette and said, "I could use a drink. Want one?"

It was close to the lunch hour and she seemed like someone who would rather not drink alone.

I followed her into the kitchen, which was nothing fancy: faded wooden cabinets, a white, four-burner stove, a small refrigerator and a Formica-topped table and two chrome legged side chairs with vinyl-padded seats. Everything had a 1950s' look. The counter held an oak knife block with seven black-handled knifes. A colander sitting in the sink held a mixture of lettuce, cherry tomatoes and what smelled like basil. She took a half-full bottle of white wine from the fridge, filled two stemmed glasses to the brim and said, "*Salute*!"

My response sent a wave of smiling wrinkles across her face.

"*Che tu possa vivere fino a cento.*" May you live to be a hundred.

"No, no," she laughed. "I don't think that's a possibility, but I don't want them pushing me in front of a bus, or running me over. Polo. You're Italian?"

"Sicilian."

She crossed her thumb over her heart. "*Ti perdono.* I forgive you. I'm Genovese."

"Who is the *them* that you mentioned?" I asked.

She gulped down half of the wine in her glass and said, "Let's go out on the deck and I'll give you all of the gory details."

CHAPTER 2

The deck was somewhere between rustic and falling down. Rotting flooring and railings, the redwood now an ash-gray color.

Overgrown coyote bushes pushed up against the deck. Four steps led down to the garden area which was filled with neglected potted plants and clumps of rosemary. It was a deep lot, going back at least a hundred feet. Privet hedges badly in need of a trim bordered the back and east side. There were six modern art concrete statues spread around the yard, ranging from three to six feet in height, two of headless semi-nude figures, the others interesting twisted figures, like musical notes slightly out of shape. Just past the porch was a cement pad, some ten foot by ten foot, partially covered with imitation lawn that had rubber golf tees inserted at the front. A golf training net with a faded bullseye in the center sat in front of the pad. Dozens of bright yellow plastic golf wiffle balls were scattered all over the yard. A white plastic five-gallon bucket held a half-dozen golf clubs.

"Are those your statues, Gaby?"

"Yes. I don't do many anymore." She flexed her fingers. "I don't have the strength."

She pointed to the sagging west-side redwood fence. “There were four towering pepper trees alongside that fence. Twenty-five feet high. Ugly things. Gaucho had them cut down. The roots were affecting the plumbing pipes and the neighbors hated them. He was planning to put in a hot tub, had the hole all dug out for it, but after he disappeared it would have been me who had to pay for it, so I just put in the golf mat.”

I set one foot on the top step but pulled back when it made loud creaking noises.

“Do you play much golf, Gaby?”

“Not anymore.” she said. “I used to be good at it. I used to be good at a lot of things.”

She cleared some newspapers from one of the two dried-out cedar Adirondack chairs and invited me to sit down.

I did so cautiously. The chair squeaked almost as loudly the stair.

“*Them* is Gaucho’s brothers, Logan and Niven.”

Gaby had said that she was eight years older than Gaucho, which would put him at sixty-six, if he was still alive.

“How old are the brothers?” I asked.

“I’m not sure. Logan’s the oldest. There was about a ten-year difference between him and Gaucho. Niven’s a year or two younger than Logan.

“Logan’s like his big brother in one way. He also married a couple of losers. The latest is an ex-Vegas showgirl, Paula. She’s in danger of dying from too many Botox injections. And there’s a weirdo that works for them named Desi. I don’t know his last name, but he is fat, ugly, and mean.

“I guess Niven was the smartest of the three. He never married.” She clicked her tongue. “His nickname was the

Gay Caballero when the Carmichael boys were drinking together or arguing, which they did a lot."

She flopped down into the chair alongside mine, balancing her wineglass in one hand. Lots of squeaks and creaks, but the chair held up.

"Here's the deal, Nick. Nine years ago, I was sick. Real sick." She fluttered some fingers at me. "They used to call it 'Big Casino' back then. If you got Big Casino you were a definite goner. The chemo treatments were terrible. My hair was falling out and my skin was the color of a clam. Christ, I was a mess. The doctors gave me six months to a year to live and I really felt that was too long. I was renting an apartment out in the Richmond District. Somehow Gaucho found out about it. Not from me, I hadn't seen or talked to him for quite some time. I was drinking and feeling really sorry for myself when the doorbell rang and there was Gaucho, holding a big bouquet of roses and singing the lyrics to that stupid old Rosemary Clooney song, *Come on-a my house, my house a come on.*

"And that's exactly what Gaucho did. He packed me and what little belongings I had and carried me right over here, to this house. He was living here, temporarily. He had just bought the place and was planning to sell it quickly. But that changed."

Gaby swirled the remaining wine around in her glass for a few seconds before taking a long sip.

"Gaucho paid for all my doctor bills and had a nurse on call for me twenty-four hours a day. At this point, he and I both thought I was a short timer, living on borrowed time. Gaucho was going through a rough divorce with Rhonda, his second wife. She was a living nightmare: a natural redhead with a beautiful face, legs that went to her shoulders, and, of course, big boobs.

"That's when he got the brainstorm about the lifetime estate contract, allowing me to stay here in this house as long as I lived. He figured that way, if I lasted until after the divorce was final, the house was safe from her, and when I died it would revert back to him and he could then sell it. So he was helping me, but also helping himself." She laughed lightly. "That was Gaucho. He always watched out for number one.

"Then God played a trick on both of us. The cancer disappeared. The doctors did all kinds of tests, but didn't come up with an explanation, other than 'good luck.' They did say that *it* could come back at any time. So I live each day as if *it* could be back tomorrow."

She waved her wineglass at me. "Come on. I need a refill and then I'll give you a tour of the house while I tell you about what happened after Gaucho disappeared."

CHAPTER 3

I saw the near empty wine bottle's label when she topped off my glass—a screw-top New Zealand Sauvignon Blanc that was in my price range—about twelve bucks.

"When did Gaucho disappear?" I asked

"Seven years ago. They found his car parked at the foot of Jefferson Street, in front of the Dolphin Club. Do you know about the club?"

I nodded my head. It was founded in 1877 and is famous for its swimming and rowing members. Especially the swimmers, who go out in the bone-chilling waters of the San Francisco Bay, most wearing nothing but a swimsuit, goggles and swim cap. A lot of police and fireman are members. John Lynch, my one-time radio car partner swam there nearly every day.

"Gaucho was a member," Gaby said. "Nobody at the Club remembered seeing him that day. The police assumed that he was there at night, after closing time. His pants, shoes, leather jacket, along with his wallet and Rolex watch were in his car."

She drained what was left of the wine into my glass and then retrieved another bottle from the fridge and handed it to me.

"You're strong enough to open it. I need to use a pair of pliers."

The wine bottle made a slight fizzy sound when I twisted off the top. It will never replace the popping of a cork.

Gaby leaned against the sink and crossed her feet. "Gaucho was a damn good swimmer. He did the Golden Gate Bridge race several times, and made it from Alcatraz back to the Dolphin Club."

She shivered slightly, folded her arms across her chest and cupped her elbows in her palms.

"I went swimming with him once. The club had a guest swim day. I'm good in the water, but the water I grew up swimming in was the on the Italian Riviera, which is some ten degrees warmer than this bay. After the swim I downed six Irish Coffees at the Buena Vista Café and I was still cold."

I handed her the wine bottle. "Was his body ever found?"

"No. The Coast Guard did a search. They said Gaucho could have drifted out the Gate or just sunk to the bottom of the bay. And that's when all hell broke loose with his family."

Her lips molded into a half smile. "Panic time. There was no suicide note. He did have a will, and that's when his brothers found out about my lifetime estate. Lawyers crawled out of the mud. Logan had one, Niven had one, both of Gaucho's ex-wives jumped into the mix. In addition to this place, Gaucho had a house and duplex in Palm Springs, and a townhouse in Vail, Colorado. And he owned a few of those storage centers, as well as a warehouse in Redwood City, and he still had some marvelous paintings, so we're talking big bucks."

"Did Gaucho have any children?"

Gaby started to smile, but stopped midway. "No. He was too selfish. He always acted like a kid himself. I guess we were both too selfish. His brother Logan had a son, but he got mixed up with drugs, was sent to prison and died there. AIDS."

She held the wine bottle over her glass for several seconds, as if she was debating on whether to pour or not. Pour won.

"So the whole gang left me alone for a while. This place was small potatoes compared to the rest."

I had been involved in a few missing person presumption of death cases. The standard length of time required by the courts in California is five years. I told that to Gaby.

"Yep. Five years. And when the time was up, even more lawyers jumped in. Gaucho was the brains of his business, GDI, Gaucho Developers, Incorporated. His brother Logan screwed everything up. He lost most of everything. He got involved in building an 'American Gated Resort Community' down near Mazatlán, Mexico. It was a big project—half of the condos had been built and sold, but Logan got in trouble with the local drug lords. They don't only control drugs down there. You buy their building materials or you're in deep trouble. They accused Logan of cooperating with the U.S. cops. They came in shooting. Tore the place up—killed several people. The project was abandoned and Logan was in deep financial doo-doo. Everyone was suing him.

"So he started coming to see me, all smiles and good wishes, his eyes going over me like a funeral director measuring for a coffin. It wasn't hard to read his mind. When is the old bitch going to take the Big Sleep? Isn't that what you private eyes call it?"

"One of them did."

"That's when I came up with the 'I'm dying as fast as I can' line. And it satisfied them for a while. But no more. Logan came by with his wife Paula and a fistful or brochures for senior assisted living places. He'd pay for everything. The brochures showed swimming pools, hot tubs, putting greens, and a lot of old farts playing cards and flashing their dentures. I'd make a lot of new friends and go on trips, instead of living alone cooped up in this old house.

"Bullshit. I know all about those places. They count your drinks and send you to bed without any tapioca dessert if you're not a good girl.

"Logan kept at it. He invited me to a party at his house, a concrete monster of a place in Redwood City. Paula picked me up in a limo and drove me down there, chatting away about how we should do lunch, go shopping. A slick salesman from the senior center was there. He had teeth like Burt Lancaster. He reminded me of that line from the song in *My Fair Lady:* 'Oozing charm from every pore, he oiled his way across the floor.' The soft sell in a hard shell. He acted like I'd kicked him in the nuts when I made it plain I didn't want anything to do with him or his old people's warehouse.

"When he left, Logan and Paula started whining, saying that as long as I lived at the house they couldn't finance any new loans, and they need money for their businesses. They told me how dangerous it was living alone, all that 'you'll fall down and never get up' crap. They walked me by this big aquarium they have right in the house. There are sharks cruising in it. Two big ones, five feet long at least. Desi, the creep, came in. He always wears a holster with a big silver gun. He was holding a bucket. He climbed a ladder and dumped some small fish into the tank. The sharks moved in and there was a feeding frenzy. Blood in the water. Desi said, 'Think what would happen if someone were to fall in there. There would be no trace of them.'"

"Why does Logan need someone like Desi around?"

"The Mexican cartel guys supposedly have a hit contract out on Logan. Desi was his security guy down in Mexico." She grunted out a laugh. "Doesn't seem like he did much of a job, does it?"

"You feel they were threatening you?"

"Damn right they were. Still are. I get all kinds of anonymous phone calls, a guy breathing, telling me how he'll use me as a sexual piñata. The doorbell rings in the middle of the night. Food that I never ordered is delivered. Rug salesmen, contractors, interior decorators come by claiming that I called for an appointment. They're trying to drive me crazy, or make it look like I am crazy, and if that doesn't work they'll run me down, break my legs or find a way to kill me."

"What about Niven?"

"I receive phone calls from Argentina or Columbia, or wherever the hell he's at. It was always the same message: move or you'll die right in this very house."

"The brothers aren't in business together?"

"They can hardly stand to be in the same room together. Niven describes himself as a South American businessman, but from what Gaucho said he was dealing drugs with some very tough characters."

She took a small sip of the wine and made a face, as if it had suddenly soured.

"Did you contact the police?"

"No. There was no way to prove it was them and if I reported it they'd make it seem that I was crazy. That's why I need you. Go see Logan. Tell him to leave me alone. Put a scare into him and Desi. You're big enough, and that face of yours looks like it's seen some action. They're getting really impatient, and I think their next move will be to kill me."

"They'd go that far?"

"Damn right. They're desperate, and they are both capable of it."

Her face was getting red and her breathing had become ragged. I tried to calm her down by getting back to Gaucho.

"Are you certain that Gaucho drowned that night?"

"The only things certain in this life are death, taxes, and lousy George Clooney movies."

She paused, breathing deeply, composing herself.

"If Gaucho was going to take his own life, I guess that's the way he would do it, in the water. He was disappointed in his father shooting himself and his hero Hemingway blowing his head off with a shotgun, rather than sailing his boat out to sea and jumping overboard.

"Gaucho inherited something from his father. He was a gambler too, but he always boasted that he was a good one. He made a lot of sport bets. Especially on the horses. 'Gaucho's the name and horses are my game' was one of his favorite lines. He used to brag about riding bareback across the Pampas in Argentina when he was a kid. He loved going to the racetracks. Sometimes we'd be across the bay at Golden Fields three times a week, or you'd be talking to him and he suddenly pull out his cell phone and talk to his bookie. One time, not long before he disappeared, we were having dinner at the Fior d' Italia, when this tough-looking giant of a man came to the table. Gaucho followed him to the bar and I saw him pass over some money. Gaucho said the guy was his bookie."

"Did Gaucho mention the man's name?"

"No. Why? Do you think you know who he is?"

"Yes, I think I may."

"Gaucho also played in those poker tournaments you see on TV, and he liked to rub shoulders at the Bellagio poker tables with guys like Mark Cuban and Leonardo DiCaprio. There were rumors that he'd lost a lot of money to some Asian mob connected guys. I know he was nervous as hell the last time I saw him. Maybe *they* dumped him in the bay."

"Contrary to what you see on TV, Gaby, the mob doesn't get rid of anyone before they collect their money."

"There's another possibility. Gaucho could have just taken off. He was doing drugs, cocaine. Right in front of me. He never did that before. I don't touch drugs, never have. Booze is my poison. He wasn't feeling well. He'd start to eat and go to the bathroom and throw up. I know Gaucho was fed up with his family and the pressures of business. If he shaved off his mustache, no one would ever recognize him. He could have stashed away a big pile of money and is now living back in Argentina. I wouldn't put it past him. That insurance investigator thought that was a possibility."

"Which insurance investigator, Gaby?"

She rubbed her chin with the rim of her wineglass. "What was his name? Forbes. Dan Forbes. Handsome young fellow. Good dresser. He had one of those neat trench coats, with the epaulets, like the British wear. He worked for...Boston Fidelity. That was it. They had to make a big payout once Gaucho was officially declared deceased, for the life insurance and the business policy Gaucho had. It was for more than three million dollars. Forbes was the one who told me about the gambling rumors."

"Who got the insurance money?"

"The brothers I guess. I know there was a lot of fighting over it."

"When was the last time you saw Gaucho?"

"A week or so before he disappeared." She jabbed a thumb up at the ceiling. "He kept some clothes in a room upstairs. Once in a while he'd stay overnight, but most of the time he spent at his place on the peninsula."

"Did you ever see Gaucho without his mustache?"

"Never. Come on, I'll show you the rest of the place."

The tour went up the stairs to the second floor, which was a hallway with a half-dozen closed doors. "My bedroom is over there, the rest of the rooms are for storage."

The third floor was interesting. One big room, taking up the entire length and width of the house, had been turned into an artist's studio. There were six large circular skylights in the ceiling and one floor to ceiling window at the street side of the room. I counted seven easels, five wooden and two of the aluminum metal tripod type. Each held a canvas that appeared to be a work in progress: seascapes, landscapes, one was a self-portrait of Gaby when she was much younger. Another with a bull charging a matador who had a huge black mustache, and another one featuring an old World War I plane disappearing into the clouds.

The floor was littered with more canvases, a couple showing the drip-splash style of Jason Pollock. Others that were a hodgepodge of different colors and textures that made me think she used them to clean her brushes.

There were small tables scattered around, covered with paint tubes and cans, as well as abalone shells that were used as ashtrays.

A Celestron refractor telescope was positioned in front of the window. If Gaby was of a mind too, she could probably zero in on the back deck of my porch, some six or seven blocks to the west.

"This is why I'm not leaving the house," Gaby said from the doorway. "It's my life. Now let me show you the basement. You'll get a kick out of it."

CHAPTER 4

It was a below ground basement that could be reached via a ramp from street level. The cement floor had a damp feel to it. A string of fluorescent fixtures bathed the room in a sickly white color.

There were four sacks of Portland cement, which I assumed were for her statue projects. Sitting on top of the cement sacks was a square-shaped cardboard box covered with colorful balloons.

I rapped a knuckle on the box. "Balloons?"

"That's a helium tank Gaucho ordered. He liked to fill up balloons and watch them take off and disappear in the sky. Red, white, and blue balloons. Very patriotic my Gaucho was."

That interested me. I had a bubble machine on my back sundeck that I used to send streams of bubbles skyward. Many of them heading off in the direction of Coit Tower. I imagined my bubbles and Gaucho's balloons smacking into each other.

There was room for three cars: a sporty white BMW coupe, a silver-blue Mercedes sedan and an unknown brand, hidden under a gray car cover. The shape made me think of something big and expensive.

"That's quite a set of cars, Gaby. Do you do much driving?"

"Never. I'm a walking or Uber girl." More butterfly fingers. "I just let some friends park here. Gaucho bought this property through a probate sale. He had someone at city hall that he bribed to get him into these deals. The former owner, Mr. Balacq, was an old bachelor, no kids or relatives. The furniture and everything else was included in the sale."

She crossed over to a wall with a single pine batten door. The area around the simple latch handle was black with grime and fingerprints.

"This is the wine cellar, Nick. When I was presented with the lifetime estate contract, it stipulated that I could use everything in the house, but I couldn't sell anything, or even take anything out of the place".

She unlatched the door, swung it open, switched on an interior light and said, "It was great while it lasted."

The interior was a neatly laid out cellar, with head-high racks of wine holding hundreds of dusty wine bottles.

"Nothing but French red wine, Nick. Three hundred and sixty bottles of the best vintages of Haut Brion, Graves, Paulliac, Rothchild, some I'd never heard of. Almost enough wine for a bottle a day for every day in a year." She smiled broadly. "I made it last twenty months."

"You drank it all?"

"Oh yeah," she said with gusto, picking out one bottle from a rack and waving it at me. The cork was inserted a half an inch or so.

"I shared some with friends. The bottles never left the house. Logan had a fit when he heard about it, but there wasn't anything he could do."

I spotted an iron floor safe at the back, of the type that Jimmy Cagney used to break into, in those old gangster movies. It was dark green in color, had a fading gold leaf inscription identifying it as from the Cary Safe Company.

"What's in the safe?" I asked.

"Nothing," Gaby said. "Gaucho had some guy come out and open it. Nothing but dust."

I twirled the combination dial. It made a nice, oily, clicking sound.

"Do you have the combination, Gaby?"

"No. I never bothered, since I have nothing to put in it."

We trooped back upstairs. I took note of the car license plates and when we were closing in on the front door, Gaby confronted me head on.

"Well, are you going to help me, Nick?"

I wanted to help her. I admired her guts and tenacity. She had survived cancer, had a sense of humor and a real enthusiasm for life. The house seemed much too big for just one person, but she didn't think so, and it somehow seemed right that she should be allowed to stay as long as she wanted.

"I think I can help you, Gaby, but I have a habit of wanting to help Nick Polo."

She tilted her head and squinted her eyes, and then the light went on.

"Oh. You need to get paid! Of course, I'm sorry."

There was a thick manila envelope lying on a small teak dresser next to the door. "Here. Three thousand dollars. That's enough to get started, isn't it?"

I peeked into the envelope. There was a neat stack of one-hundred-dollar bills, and a folded white sheet of typing paper.

I removed ten of the bills and the paper, then dropped the envelope back on the dresser. "This is fine for now."

"I wrote down Logan Carmichael's address and phone number," she said. "His wife lives with him. I don't know about Desi. I have no idea where Niven is living or how to get in touch with him."

She leaned over and plucked a brass-headed golf putter from a large galvanized milk can that had been converted into an umbrella stand, and that's when I realized where I'd seen her before, walking around North Beach, going to some of the same bakeries and butchers that I did. She had worn a big floppy hat and sunglasses, so I never saw her face. But she always seemed to have that golf putter in one hand.

"I walk every day, Nick. When you get to be my age, you either walk or you die. My balance isn't what it was, and I don't want to be seen like an old lady with a cane, so I use the putter. In the past two weeks, there have been guys on bicycles zipping close by me, close enough to nearly make me fall. And just two days ago one of those big black SUVs came really close to me as I was crossing the street."

She waved the putter around like a sword. "I took a swipe at it and put a dent by the right rear door."

"Did you notice at the license plate?"

"No. It was going real fast and my eyes aren't that good anymore, but I wouldn't be surprised if it was Logan or Desi."

"Your walks. Do you always walk around the same time, and take the same route?"

She drummed the putter head on the floor. "I usually take a short walk in the morning, then work in the studio until the early afternoon, then have a nap and take off about three o'clock, post lunch and pre-dinner time, when it's not too crowded and you can get an espresso or a seat at a bar. I take different walks; sometimes down to Fisherman's Wharf, or Union Square, the Ferry Building, but mostly around North Beach. Wherever I'm in a mood to go."

I dug one of my business cards out of my wallet. It listed my name, phone number, email address, PI license number, but no address. I printed the address in big bold letters on the back of the card.

"I live just a few blocks from here, so call me if you have any trouble. I'll be out in front at three o'clock. Take your walk around North Beach today. If you spot Logan or this Desi fellow, wave the putter over your head, okay?"

"Okay."

There's always something that seems to slip your mind, and when I had my hand on the doorknob it dawned on me. "What about a burglar alarm, Gaby? Or security cameras."

She made a one shoulder shrug. "I had an alarm system put in years ago, at the estate's expense. It went off accidentally a few times and scared the living hell out of me. Sirens, cops showing up at the door. I couldn't get to sleep worrying that I had left a window or something open and the damn thing would go off again, so I got rid of it."

It was an all too common problem—alarm syndrome. A professional, and very successful burglar that I'd arrested more than once, told me that he counted on fifteen to twenty percent of targeted houses to never have their systems activated.

"Do you feel safe living here alone?"

She shrugged with her eyebrows. "I had two lovely dogs. Cocker Spaniels. Merlo and Pinot. They both died, and I'm too old to handle a new one. I've got a hunting rifle in my bedroom, and I keep my pistol close by."

Gaby crossed over to the teak dresser, slid out a drawer and came out with a small revolver with pearl handles.

"I've had it for years. I took it along to Africa and the Caribbean with Gaucho. I'm a good…I used to be a pretty good shot." She threw in a short chuckle. "I remember Gaucho's advice: 'Shoot first and call whatever you hit the target.'"

She kept the barrel pointed to the ground and her forefinger outside the trigger guard.

"Gaby, if you take the gun along with you on one of your walks and the police stop you, you'll be in a lot of trouble."

"I know, I know. It's a house gun. But if anyone comes in here without my permission, he's in for a big surprise."

CHAPTER 5

At a quarter to three that afternoon I cruised by Gaby Maoret's house. Hers was the only single-family dwelling. The rest were all apartment houses, tightly packed together, most a little the worse for wear, with cars parked in the driveway and on the sidewalks.

Ah, the streets of San Francisco. There used to be a police procedural TV series under that name, with the great Karl Malden and Michael Douglas, when he was very young. I enjoy seeing a rerun now and then because you can actually see the streets, and the curbs.

Not anymore. The city has become a driving-parking nightmare. Road rage over an open parking spot often leads to bloodshed. Parking is done bumper-to-bumper, making getting out of that spot difficult, and, once the space is open, three or four cars zoom in to claim it. There is some civility in the daytime when the meter maids are buzzing about, but after dark it gets dangerous. The local newspaper had a recent headline: Car Break-ins Now a Steady Circumstance. It happens, get used to it. The cops don't even bother to respond to calls about the break-ins anymore. "Notify your insurance carrier" is their solution.

I avoided a lot of this for a long time by driving what a

lady friend called my Polomobile—a dusty, beat up old tan sedan with a whip antenna. It looked exactly like a police undercover car, the windshield sticker proclaiming SFPD HOMOCIDE added to allusion.

But even that doesn't work anymore. There simply are very few *illegal* parking spots available. All of the red zones, fire hydrants and bus stops are taken over.

There are a good number of disabled person spots, painted blue, for those in need. Unfortunately, a lot of those not in need were making use of them. One local physician was known as "Dr. Parker" because he passed out the needed medical documents to obtain a disabled placard from the DMV to anyone with the money to pay his bill.

So the Polomobile stays in the garage a good deal of the time while I tool around on a Suzuki sports motorcycle. I had been a solo motorcycle cop for fourteen months before being transferred to the Inspector's Bureau. We rode big Harley Davidson Road Kings. The department brought in the little Suzukis to patrol Golden Gate Park and to use in parades. I bought mine at a police auction, so it still has the blue seven-point star with the letters SFPD printed in gold star decals on both sides. I cover them with saddlebags when it's not parked. So far, eleven months and no parking tickets.

I just use it for short, in-town trips. The only downside is that a bike limits your wardrobe and the helmet is a pain to lug around so I usually just lock it to the handlebar.

Gaby Maoret popped out of her front door right at three o'clock. She was wearing a tan, straw-woven floppy hat with a broad brim, sunglasses with lenses the size of coffee saucers and a khaki, multi-pocketed safari-style jacket. No purse. Whatever she needed was in the jacket's pockets. I hoped her pearl handled revolver wasn't amongst them. She swung the golf putter around rhythmically, back and forth in a low arc, a conductor warming up for a concert.

It was a nice afternoon for a walk: temperature in the high sixties, no wind, the sky tinted a brassy-saffron color due to an out of control forest fire up in Mendocino County, some one hundred fifty miles north of the city. The terrible fires were becoming an annual event, with seemingly no end in sight.

Gaby took a leisurely stroll down the Greenwich Street hill and entered North Beach, the city's "Little Italy." The Italian influence was becoming littler by the day as Asian, and even a few Irish bars and restaurants moved in.

She turned left on Grant Avenue and made her way to the Caffe Trieste on Stockton, once known as the home of the Bohemian Culture, for her cup of espresso. She had a window seat all to herself. No one bothered her.

Then she was up and moving north on Columbus Avenue for a couple of blocks, taking her time, stopping to glance at store windows, giving anyone following her plenty of time to keep up.

Her next stop was Gino & Carlo's Cocktail Lounge on Green Street. Actually it's not a lounge, it's a bar—a 6 a.m. to 2 a.m. bar that's home to locals, including fisherman, cops, firemen and bread truck drivers. Word of mouth about the reasonable prices and friendly bartenders bring in fresh crops of tourists.

Gaby settled herself on a stool and chatted with the bartender as he prepared her drink, a Maker's Mark Manhattan in a stemmed glass with two cherries, while Sinatra invited everyone to "Come Fly with Me" in the background.

I nursed a beer and watched as a middle-aged man wearing a Giants windbreaker and jeans sat down next to her and started up a conversation. When Gaby took off her sunglasses and tapped the putter on the edge of the bar I moved in close. I couldn't hear what kind of a pitch he was making, but I did catch her eloquent last line: "Fuck off, buddy."

When she finished her drink she made a final stop at Victoria Pastry for a box of biscottis, and then trekked back to the house. No one bothered her, no one even came close.

I waited a few minutes then knocked on her door.

She opened the door wide and dance-stepped backwards. "Want a cookie?"

"No thanks, Gaby, I'm going to take off. Call me if anyone tries to bother you. I'm going down to see Gaucho's brother in the morning. I'll let you know what happens."

Her Manhattan seemed to have made an impression on her. She slurred her words a bit when she said, "Kick 'em in the balls for me."

I had one more stop to make before heading home.

I wheeled the Suzuki up on the sidewalk near the Saxxe Realty office on Beach Street. It was close enough to Fisherman's Wharf to hear the sea lions barking near Pier 39.

There were more than a dozen cubicle offices on the first floor. Kaye Palmer's was at the rear of a long corridor.

"Nick, it's so good to see you," she beamed, once I was in her space. She gave me a big hug. She was an excellent hugger: full body contact from knees to neck, and all of the spots in between.

Kaye was on either side of fifty, her hair was auburn. She had wide, mocha-colored eyes and she was dressed all in beige, shirt, blouse and jacket. Gucci emblems popped up on her belt, scarf, and wristwatch.

When she settled back behind her desk she said, "Tell me, Nick. Is it good news? Is that crazy old lady finally moving out?" She brought her hands together in a prayer-like gesture. "I hope she hasn't passed away."

Kaye was talking about Mrs. Damonte, my one and only tenant, a formidable, feisty woman who considers herself to be a *strega,* an Italian witch with magical powers. I'd inherited a pair of flats from my parents when they died in an airline crash many years ago. Mrs. Damonte has been living in the bottom flat since I was a little kid.

"No. She's alive and kicking," I said.

I had done a small job for Kaye. One of her client's tenants had disappeared, owing thousands in rent, and taking everything that was not nailed down in the house when he left. I found him living in a trailer park in Napa. She was grateful, and stopped by my place with a check and a bottle of wine, and ran into Mrs. D while she was giving the basement floor its daily Pine Sol bath. Mrs. D goes through Pine Sol the way Pizza Hut goes through tomato sauce.

She's very suspicious of any woman who comes visiting, because she fears I'll get married, and sell the flats. When she found out that Kaye was a Realtor, she started spouting curses in Italian and giving her the *maloocchio*—the evil eye.

Kaye picked up a pen and scribbled a figure on a Post-it notepad, tore off the page and handed it to me.

"This is what I can get you for renting or leasing out the flat, Nick."

I groaned inwardly. The monthly figure she'd written down was more than triple what Mrs. Damonte paid for an entire year.

"And I remember that you have a full basement. You could rent out parking spaces at four hundred a month per car."

Then Kaye twisted another knife deep into my financial heart.

"If you want to sell, this is what I can get you. Tomorrow. I've got clients who will jump at it."

This time I groaned out loud. "Not now, Kaye. But maybe soon. I wanted to talk to you about another house."

I gave her the address on Greenwich.

Her hand darted over and grabbed mine. "Gaucho Carmichael's place! Is it for sale? What do you know that I don't? It's been tied up in court for years."

"So you know all about it?"

"Every Realtor in the city knows about that house."

"What's the house worth?"

"Nothing," she snorted. "The first thing you'd do is tear the house down. The property is where the value is. The zoning would let you go up nine stories, and it all depends on what the builders chose to do; maybe a mixture of studio and one-bedroom condos on the first few floors, and then start expanding to larger, luxury units up higher. It's a gold mine, Nick."

"I was just there, Kaye. The lady in residence has a lifetime estate contract and she's not interested in giving it up."

"If I was the owner, I'd make her an offer she couldn't refuse. A big, fat financial offer. Would it bother you if I approached her? I wouldn't mention that I spoke to you."

"No. But I think you'd be wasting your time, and I can't give you her name, Kaye."

"You don't have to. Her name and that of the property

owner will be on the court documents."

"Speaking of the owner, I'd like to know more about him."

She swiveled her chair towards her computer. "Do you want me to run a title check on him and the property?"

I wanted.

CHAPTER 6

Mrs. Damonte was taking off for a wake when I got back to the flats. A day without a wake is like a day without sunshine for Mrs. D.

She was always dressed for that particular occasion in one of her Frederick's of the Vatican outfits: black dress, black wool coat and back converse tennis shoes. All she had to do was pop on a black pillbox funeral hat with a down-to-the-chin veil and she was all set. She's somewhere between eighty-five and ninety-five, and is less than five feet tall.

We converse mainly in Italian. She knows a little Spanish and I'm sure that she understands more of the English language than she lets on. The closest she comes to using English is "Nopa" for a negative response; "Shita" when she's angry; and a clear as a bell "Bingo!" when the occasion arises.

She'd left me a steaming plate of *bottarga,* which translates as smoked eggs from the rat of the sea. It's also known as Sicilian caviar. The roe from gray mullets are salted, pressed and then left in the air to dry for six months, turning it into a solid hunk of eggs the color of amber. Mrs. D sautés it in oil and garlic then adds it to pasta. Fantastic.

I spent the evening going over the real estate reports that Kaye Palmer had provided. The Greenwich Street house was listed as a life estate deed with Logan and Niven Carmichael as joint remaindermen.

Kaye had scribbled in some notes which indicated that once Gaby was gone, the house reverted to the Carmichael brothers. She underlined the notation stating, "This does not mean there won't be further legal action by others."

Logan Carmichael's property in Redwood City was under his name only, and had an assessed value of just under four million dollars, which in California meant a bite of forty thousand dollars in yearly taxes. I guess if you can afford a four-mil house, the bite doesn't hurt too much.

I ran Logan and Niven Carmichael through a few web sites. Logan had numerous listings for property liens. Niven was a no show. There were dozens of hits on the disaster at the resort gated community in Mexico. There had indeed been a bloodbath, with eleven men, most of them laborers working on the site, shot to death. The condos were riddled with machine gun fire and graffiti spray painted with *Regala de Los Zetos,* The Los Zetos rule. There were no arrests, and one story said that the local police had had a good view of the entire incident, staying well back while the shooting went on.

Several stories popped up on Gaucho, including articles from the *San Francisco Chronicle* on his disappearance. All of the photos showed him with that big mustache.

Gaby Maoret garnered a lot of press, mostly all about her career as a teacher at the San Francisco Art Institute, and her skill as an artist. There were photos of her with works on display at art galleries around the Bay Area. Gaucho could be seen lurking in the background in some of the pictures.

I decided to wait until meeting with Logan before running him and Niven through my favorite databases.

Nine o'clock on a Sunday morning is a nice time for a drive down to Redwood City, which is just thirty miles south of San Francisco, and often thirty degrees warmer in temperature. It got its name due to the fact that in the 1850s redwood trees were harvested from hills a few miles to the west and sent down a creek to the harbor.

The city slogan used to be Climate Best by Government Test. Now they're pushing the Start of Silicon Valley. The way things are moving, the Start of Silicon Valley will soon be South San Francisco.

I wanted to catch Logan Carmichael while he was likely to be at his house, which was located at 713 Bay Road, in an area of the city called Friendly Acres, a mix of residences and businesses: auto body shops, small factories, mini-storage facilities, junk yards and burrito places, just west of the Bayshore Freeway. Stanford University, along with Google, Facebook and the usual suspects, were buying up large tracks of land for expansion.

There was a .38 snub-nosed revolver secreted in the Polomobile's passenger side headrest, but I wanted to be fully dressed when meeting the Carmichaels, so I had a 9mm Sig Saur semiautomatic in a shoulder holster under my left arm. With the zipper of my windbreaker open, you couldn't miss seeing the gun. Sometimes in this business it pays to advertise.

Gaby had described Logan's building as a 'concrete monster of a place' and that was an apt description. It looked as if it had been put together by a kid playing

LEGO with giant reinforced concrete blocks in a variety of tints and textures. Long and wide, two stories high. The second-floor windows were deep and narrow in the thick walls, like the ones they shoot arrows through in the movies. The ones on the ground floor were eight feet high and covered with a mirror-like silver reflective film.

The building was set back some fifty yards from the street. A rusty, lurching anchor chain fence, propped up by two-by-four pieces of lumber in spots, guarded the entire perimeter, with a break for a cantilevered steel security gate in the entranceway. A small black callbox had a bright red button under a placard that read: Push to Talk.

I pushed. I talked.

I didn't know how Logan Carmichael would react if I just hit him straight about my working for Gaby, so I decided to use a pretext involving Gaucho's death.

"This is Nick Polo, I'm an insurance investigator. I have some information regarding Ethan Carmichael."

There was no vocal response, but after two minutes had ticked by the gate opened with a screech of metallic pain.

The ground surface was covered with large rectangular patches of various paving materials: plain concrete, pebbles, cobblestones, granite, flagstone and travertine.

A dust-covered bright yellow John Deere Bobcat bulldozer sat against the far fence wall.

The only touch of greenery was a lone cactus plant of the shape and size of the one Spike, Snoopy's brother, hung out around in the Peanut's cartoons.

A cream-colored Lincoln Continental, a black Cadillac Escalade SUV, and a battered red Toyota pickup truck with the initials GDI, for Gaucho Development Incorporated, stenciled on its sides were positioned on the east side of the house.

I parked next to the Escalade. There was a two-inch dent, the paint scraped away, on the back right side, where Gaby said she'd slammed the SUV with her putter.

There was no sign of surveillance cameras and the two blue and white ADT alarm signs were faded to the point of almost being unreadable. Apparently Logan was no longer worried about a visit from the Mexican cartels.

A serpentine paved concrete path painted the purple color of a bruise led to a copper-clad door, which was yanked open while I was searching for the doorbell.

A short, thick-set man with heavy shoulders, a melon gut and a round face with an accordion of double chins glared at me. His eyes were lost in the heavy ridges of his face, like raisins thumbed into cookie dough. His crow-black hair was jelled to the stiffness of porcupine quills. He had a crushed nose and deeply pocked skin. He was wearing a faded black polo with the GDI crest on the chest and low-slung jeans with a belt too large, its unused portion hung down in front of his fly. The black nylon holster on his right hip held a large chrome revolver with stag horn grips. He had a red stained white towel draped over one shoulder and a meat cleaver in his meaty right hand.

I guessed that he was Desi, whom Gaby had described as being big, ugly, and mean. You could call him ugly if you were unkind. You could also do so if you were being honest.

"What's with you?" he asked, in a whiny, sing-song voice that didn't go along with his frame.

"What's with the meat cleaver, Desi?"

"You know me?"

"We haven't been formally introduced," I said, opening the windbreaker so that he could see the Sig Saur. "I'd like to talk to Carmichael. Is he in?"

He patted the cleaver against his leg and smiled, showing a surprising set of bright white teeth.

"Nice gun, but mine is bigger."

"But I bet it goes off half-cocked a lot."

His mouth paused for a moment, as though he was considering or rejecting a thought, then he said, "It's feeding time. Come on in."

I followed him inside. The walls and ceilings appeared to be of concrete, all tinted in various shades of copper, brown and a deep red hue. The floor, when it wasn't covered with throw rugs, was black and shiny, like a deep lake.

"Hey, Logan," Desi squealed. "That guy is here."

A mid-sized man dressed in khaki cargo shorts and a Tommy Bahama-style shirt featuring palm trees and pineapples walked up to within a couple of feet of me. He had a rounded back and caved-in stomach. His hair was mouse-colored and wavy. There was a thin mustache above his lip that looked like it had been drawn with a pencil. He had pale gray eyes and for some reason his forehead was greasy with perspiration.

"Who are you? And what's this shit about my brother?"

I handed him a business card. "I'm an insurance investigator, Mr. Carmichael. We have reason to believe that Ethan is alive."

"Ethan? No one ever calls him that."

He reached over and tapped a forefinger against my chest, pulling it back quickly when it made contact with the gun.

"Gaucho died years ago. The probate is all over. Settled. What are you guys trying to do? Get the insurance money back?"

"Not a chance," Desi said, still holding onto the cleaver.

"There have been sightings of a man in Argentina. He is using a different name, but he reportedly told a woman that he was actually Ethan Carmichael."

"That's crazy," Logan said. "What name was he using?"

"George Kaplan," I said, dredging up a character's name from an old Alfred Hitchcock film. "He matches the description of your brother; however, without the mustache. He is apparently not in the best of health."

He waved my business card under my nose. "This says that you're a private investigator."

"I work for several different insurance companies. Would you be willing to supply us with a DNA sample, Mr. Carmichael? A lock of hair, or I could provide you with a DNA swab kit."

He threw my card onto the floor and stamped around in an angry circle.

There were heel clicks on the concrete floor. It's funny how you can usually tell when those clicks belong a beautiful woman.

She was tall and blonde, with long tan arms and long tan legs showcased by a pair of tight white booty shorts and a butter-yellow square neck tank top. Her eyes were pale blue and narrow, like a cat's. Her bright red lips were slightly swollen and her face looked a little tight, as if she'd gone back for that second facelift a little too soon. Or maybe Gaby was right, and the lady was overdoing the Botox injections.

The shoes that had made all that clicking noise were black high heel platform sandals.

"What's all the shouting about, Logan?" she asked, her voice low-pitched and nasally.

"This joker is a private investigator. He says that Gaucho

is alive."

"I'm Paula," she said, holding out a hand.

"Have any of you heard from Ethan since he allegedly disappeared?"

"He's dead," Logan wailed. "Drowned in the bay. This is all bullshit."

"I need a cup of coffee," Paula said. "How about you Mr.—?"

"Nick Polo. I'd love one."

I followed her into the kitchen, a modern affair with granite countertops and stainless-steel appliances. There was an eight-foot-long walnut butcher block center island, the top littered with knives, pots and a plastic container holding a dozen or more fish. My father had been a fishmonger and I had worked the crab boats when I was a kid, so I recognized the rock cod, scorpion fish, groupers, and red snappers.

Desi went to work with his meat clever on the fish while Paula poured me a cup of coffee from a machine that looked like a small robot from a *Star Wars* movie.

"I'm going to contact my attorney," Logan said. "You people just can't waltz in here and drop this bullshit on my lap."

"I understand you've been spending a great deal of time with your attorneys, Mr. Carmichael."

He hitched up his shorts and said, "What the hell does that supposed to mean?"

"Nothing. Just that the home office indicated you were involved in current litigation."

Hang around with lawyers long enough and you end up talking like them. The statement had an immediate effect on Logan Carmichael.

"Now listen to me, asshole. I don't——"

"Let's just all relax," Paula interjected smoothly. "Mr. Polo, is there any real proof that Gaucho is alive?"

"No, there is not."

"Then aren't we getting ahead of things? I find it hard to believe that he would just show up after all these years."

"It's bullshit!" Logan said. He seemed to say that a lot.

Paula settled down on a chrome-legged black leather kitchen stool and crossed her long, curvy legs.

"Nick. Can I call you Nick?"

She had the kind of figure that allowed her to call men anything she wanted. I nodded my head.

"Nick. What's in this for you? I mean, do you work on a salary, or do you get a commission if you actually find Gaucho?"

"Just a salary."

That brought a smile to those puffy lips. "And I bet they're not paying you what you're worth."

I pasted a stupid grin on my face. I'm good at that.

"Maybe we could work together," Paula said. "You keep us posted as to what's going on and we'll make sure you get your just rewards."

I gave the ceiling and walls an admiring glance. "This is an interesting house. That's a lot of cement."

"Concrete," Logan said. "It's not just freeways and cellblocks anymore, it's the future, pal. Rock solid, and can withstand floods and fires."

"And it's sexy," Paula said, making a show of re-crossing her legs.

"I've got big jobs lined up all over Silicon Valley," Logan said as he hitched up his belt.

"Chow time," Desi said, picking up a plastic bucket full

of fish parts and holding it over his head as if it were a trophy.

We all followed him down a hallway to an area with three steps leading to a large room with a sunken floor. I had to stop and make sure I was seeing what I was seeing. A glass-walled aquarium stretched across the room. An L-shaped maroon stuffed leather couch and four matching club chairs were spaced around the room. While I was standing there with my mouth open, Paula edged in and slipped her arm under my elbow.

"Isn't this something, Nick? Twenty-thousand gallons of saltwater."

The water was a clear blue-gray color. There were rock tunnels and clumps of seaweed in colors ranging from bright orange to pale green, their bands waving back and forth like marginata plants do in the wind.

A pair of bright yellow tang fish, the size and thickness of my hand, darted by.

Desi moved to the end of the room. The top of the tank could only be reached by a pro basketball center. There was an aluminum step ladder braced against the side wall.

Logan Carmichael walked up to the aquarium wall and rapped his knuckles against the glass.

"We've got a couple of leopard sharks, some California sting rays, tang fish, and purple lobsters." He rapped his knuckles against the glass again and a shark some four or five feet in length undulated by. It had a yellow brown skin tone with dark brown colored bars draped across its back and dark spots along its side. And a pair of beady black doll's eyes.

Desi climbed up the wall and used a pair of tongs to dangle a piece of fish into the water. The shark made a beeline for the fish. Desi began dropping more fish into the water and a second shark joined in. Desi then dumped the entire bucket into the water and a feeding frenzy began.

"Look at them go at it," Logan said, clapping his hands as if applauding for a rock band.

Paula was staring at the spectacle, her tongue darting around her lips.

"I don't get it," I said. "What's the sense of all of this? The aquarium must cost a fortune."

"Damn right it does," Logan said. "And we're going to make a fortune selling them. It's the new thing. People with money are tired of dogs, cats, swimming pools and little aquariums. You get one of these are you're in the lead. It's like watching *Jaws* in your own house."

Paula piped in with, "They are the sexiest animals in the world."

Sexy. Like in concrete.

Logan moved in tight, almost pressing his nose against the glass. "These are small sharks. They can get to be up to eight or nine feet, but I'm working on getting a Blacktip Reef Shark or Tiger Shark. That'd really be something.

"I've got a fisherman in Half Moon Bay who supplies me with live cod and sand dabs. I use them when I'm showing the aquarium to customers. Man, you should see them when the sharks go at it." He brought his hands together in a loud clap. "They go crazy. Can't wait to give me an order."

My thoughts on sharks trapped in an aquarium were the same as on tigers, lions, all of the big cats, fenced in at a zoo. They were all magnificent animals who should be left alone and allowed to roam free.

"Where do you get the sharks?" I asked.

“There’s a shark supply dealer down in Los Angeles,” Logan said. “He gets them out by Catalina Island. We’re getting two new ones delivered in a couple of days. These guys are getting dull and lazy.”

“So what will you do with them?”

Logan made a slashing across his throat gesture. “Desi butchers them, puts them in the freezer, and then we feed the meat to the new guys. They’re cannibals.”

Desi climbed down from the ladder, holding the bucket precariously in front of him. Some fish blood had spilled onto his shirt. I felt like asking him to take a swim.

We moved back to the kitchen. Desi took a Heineken beer bottle from a huge stainless-steel refrigerator and twisted off the top.

He didn’t offer anyone to join him, and I could have used a beer. Somehow watching the three of them drooling at the sight of the shark feed had upset my stomach.

“What about your brother, Niven?” I asked.

Logan scratched at his mustache with his thumb. “Niven is a loser. He dropped a fortune in Venezuela and Argentina, and then he tried to get me to give him some money for flower farms in Columbia.” He grunted out a laugh. “Flowers!”

“Have you seen him lately?”

“No. And I don’t intend do.”

“You may have to. He has half interest in Gaucho’s remaining estate, doesn’t he?”

I was getting under Logan’s ruddy skin.

He tugged at his zipper. “What’s that to you? You’re poking your nose where it doesn’t belong.”

Desi wasn’t all that happy with me either.

“You should get the fuck out of here, before I throw

you out."

Paula's high heels made clicking noises and she hurried over to stand between Desi and me.

"Let's all be civil, boys. Remember, we want to work together on this."

"I spoke to Gabriela Maoret yesterday," I said.

Logan rocked back on his heels. "Gaby? That old bitch. What are you talking to her for?"

"She was friendly with your brother, and was one of the last persons to see him alive."

"God, I hate that woman! Do you know how much money she's costing me?"

Paula did her calm-down-boys act. "Now Logan. I'm sure Nick was right in talking to Gaby." She batted her baby blues at me.

"It's true, though. She is living in that great big house all by herself. It's a waste. And dangerous. You read all the time about these poor old women who fall down in the kitchen and lay there for days until they die."

Desi threw in his medical advice. "Or slip in the tub and drown."

Logan walked over to the massive French door refrigerator and grabbed a Heineken. He couldn't pop the top like Desi had. Paula fished an opener from a kitchen drawer for him.

"I've been trying to help that old bat for years," Logan said, after he helped himself to a swig of the beer. "I tried to put her in a nice place, really nice, with people her own age. But she's just too damn hardheaded. Did she tell you how much money I offered her? A half a million dollars! And there's the painting. Did she tell you about that?"

"Which painting?"

Logan held out the beer bottle. "Some oil on canvas piece of crap by Ellsworth Kelly that Gaucho bought before he disappeared. It's just a blob of green paint the color of this bottle on a plain white background. Gaucho paid six hundred thousand for it! It never turned up. I think that old bitch has it hidden somewhere in the house."

"Maybe you could talk to her again, Nick" Paula purred. "I'm sure my husband would be grateful if you could...explain things to her. We're afraid that she's gotten senile."

"It didn't seem that way to me," I said. "She seems fine. She's still painting, cooking, walking. I like her. I like her a lot. And as it happens I live very close to her. I'd hate to see anything happen to Gaby, like some jerk knocking her down or running her over."

There was what could be described as a pregnant pause, and then Desi slammed the meat cleaver on the butcher block, Logan hitched up his shorts, and Paula gave me a disappointed look.

Desi started walking right at me, the cleaver in his hand,

We locked eyes. I folded the windbreaker open and said, "Put it down. Now."

He hesitated long enough to make him feel like he was winning our staring contest, then threw the cleaver on the counter. It bounced around and clattered down to the floor.

"You'll lose your edge that way, Desi," I said.

"Fuck you!" was his predictable response.

Paula and Logan stayed put, but Desi followed me right out to the front door.

He stood in the doorway for a few moments, shoulders hunched, feet spread apart, hands on hips, neck bowed, doing a pretty good impression of a bull, huffing and puffing like he was getting ready to blow the house down.

When I reached my car he walked over and stuck his foot on the Polomobile's front bumper.

"This piece of shit yours?"

"Bought and paid for."

He patted his hand on the Escalade's hood. "This is mine, and again, it's bigger than yours. You married?"

"Why? Are you looking for a date?"

That got me a mouthful of teeth.

"You visit us, maybe I'll come by and visit you, huh?"

I got in the car and started the engine. He was still staring at me, his right hand gripping and regripping the revolver.

"Be careful you don't shoot yourself with that gun, Desi. Have you got a permit for it? You get heavy jail time around here for carrying without a permit."

I gave him a friendly wave as I drove off. Once again his response was predictable: a one finger wave.

CHAPTER 7

When I got back home, I nosed the Polomobile into the flat's garage. It was a big garage, capable of housing my car, the motorcycle and three or four more vehicles, of the type that according to Kay Palmer, would pay up to four hundred dollars a month rent.

A sound coming from the backyard caught my attention. Mrs. Damonte laughing. I'd heard her cackling all my life, but this was a loud, happy laugh.

She and Gaby Maoret were wandering around Mrs. D's vegetable garden, speaking in Italian, both of them using their hands a lot. Mrs. D was wearing black sweats and rubber rain boots that reached up above her knees. Gaby was in her safari jacket and big floppy hat.

The garden contained a cornucopia of vegetables, most of which she sold to a couple of nearby restaurants: cima de rapa, several varieties of tomatoes, leeks, zucchini the size of footballs, cauliflower, eggplant, three colors of bell peppers, a dozen or more herb plants, and a semi-dwarf cherry tree, all laid out neatly, and, protected by Mrs. D's vigilance and home-brewed insect repellents. She relied on her Red Ryder BB rifle to frighten away birds and neighborhood cats who were foolish enough to wander into her kingdom.

It dawned on me that the two of them had something in common: They were both Genovese. Gaby's lover and benefactor had disappeared into San Francisco Bay, and Mrs. Damonte's husband, a crab boat fisherman, had sailed away under the Golden Gate Bridge some thirty years ago, and, like Gaucho, was eventually pronounced dead. I didn't believe it. I think he just wanted to get away from Mrs. D and is living happily ever after. Who knows? Maybe the two of them were sharing a bottle of wine on a sunny beach somewhere.

Gaby spotted me, raised an arm and shouted "Hello."

Mrs. D gave Gaby a farewell nod and said, "*E'stato un piacere conoscerti.*" It was nice to meet you.

She gave me the evil eye: "*Sei tornado.*" You're back.

Gaby said, "I had to come by and see you. I heard from Gaucho this morning, or someone who claimed to be Gaucho."

"What happened?"

"The phone rang, I picked it up and there was this voice. It sounded like him, but it was a terrible connection. The line was crackling and breaking up."

"What time was this?" I asked.

She glanced at her wristwatch. "About nine o'clock."

Mrs. D was close by, picking tomatoes, bell peppers and leeks, her head cocked so she wouldn't miss a word of our conversation.

"What did he say?"

"That he had been very sick and almost died. That he still loved me and wished that he could see me again."

I grabbed her by the elbow and led her over to the green woven metal bench perched under the cherry tree. It was a brand-new bench, the kind you see at bus stops. One of

Mrs. D's cronies had a nephew who worked for the Muni. "*Eccedeza, non ne hanno bisogno.*" Surplus—they no need, she claimed.

Maybe so, but every time the doorbell rang I expected a couple of muni employees and a cop to make inquiries about a missing bench.

"Do you really think it was Gaucho?"

She settled down on the bench and squeezed her knees together.

"I don't know. I asked why he hadn't contacted me before, and he said that he was worried that somehow someone could trace him to where he was living now."

"Did he say where that was?"

"No. And I asked. He did call me by a nickname he had for me: *Fierabras.* Spitfire. I could hear someone in the background, singing. In Spanish. Argentinian Spanish."

"They speak a different Spanish in Argentina?"

"Oh, yes, the Argentinian accent is a different beast from Mexico or the rest of South America. They speak with the sing-song rhythm that many Italians use."

It was my turn to sit down and squeeze my knees together. Why the hell would Gaucho suddenly pop up now?

"What else did he say, Gaby?"

"Not much. There was a commotion. Footsteps. Doors slamming. 'Gotta go,' he said, and then he broke the connection."

"Did you record the conversation?"

"No. I'm not smart enough for a smart phone. All I have is an old laptop computer and my landline. There's no answering machine anymore. The old one broke and I'm too lazy to install another one, so there was no way to record it. I knew you'd want to know about the call, so I walked over here and Ludovica was nice enough to invite me inside."

"Ludovica?"

"Yes." She pointed to Mrs. Damonte. "*La padrona di casa.*"

The woman of the house! I had known that woman all of my life and never heard her first name.

"Who else knew about this *Fierabras* nickname for you?"

"Everyone who ever heard us having an argument, and that certainly included his brothers and their wives."

"I just came back from talking with Logan Carmichael, Gaby."

I gave her a rundown on what had taken place.

"Do you think he'll leave me alone now?" she asked, tapping her putter-cane on the used brick path that curved through the garden.

"I hope so," I said. And hope was all I had. Logan was the kind of guy who could be handled, but Desi was a different breed. One of those hardheaded macho types who kept getting up after you knocked them to the floor. I was afraid that he'd do something stupid and then I'd have to put him down hard.

"Logan told me he offered you a half a million dollars to move out of the house."

"Words. Nothing on paper, and once the offer gets on paper, there will be all kinds of contingencies before I see any money."

"Logan also mentioned that Gaucho had purchased a valuable painting just before he disappeared."

"Oh, that," she sighed, leaning back on the bench. "The Ellsworth Kelly abstract. It's titled Green on White 71. Gaucho asked me about it. I thought he paid too much."

"Where is it now?"

"It could be anywhere. Gaucho was planning to wash it as soon as he could, or use it to pay off some debts."

Gaby peered up into the cherry tree. "It's a simple way of washing money. You owe someone, oh, say a million dollars. The movement of the money via a bank transfer falls right into the IRS computers. Taxes galore. So, you do a 'Picasso Float.' They named the technique after Picasso because he was always worth money, whether it was a painting, a sculpture, a collage or some scribbling on a restaurant tablecloth. Of course the person owed the money would have to be into art. But these people usually have all the money they need, and what would you rather look at? A bank statement or a Picasso?"

"This painting that Gaucho bought, what's it worth?"

"Ellsworth Kelly is an established abstract artist. Once you're established you've got it made. And he's dead. There will be no more Kellys. His paintings have sold for big money at auctions, for between three and four million dollars."

"What do you think of his work?" I asked.

"Well, if you wanted to forge a painting, he'd be a top choice. Most are simple abstract geometrics of two or three colors. The one Gaucho picked up was relatively small, about three feet by four feet. A lot of Kelly's works are of a much larger size, ten by ten, some bigger."

"Could it have been a forgery?"

"Not to my eye. And I trust my eye, Nick. His initials EK, and the canvas number 71 are on the front right, and Kelly is written on the stretcher. The provenance is from the Janus gallery in New York City, and they are top of the line."

There was a series of plinking-coughing sounds and Gaby jumped to her feet, raising the putter over her shoulder.

"What's was that?"

I pointed to Mrs. Damonte, who had her Red Ryder BB gun in her hands, shooting up toward the sky, where a flock of wild cherry-headed parrots suddenly turned in a flight in a close-wing pattern worthy of the Blue Angels and headed back toward Telegraph Hill.

"My God," Gaby gasped. "Ludovica isn't trying to kill the parrots is she?"

The wild parrots have become a tourist attraction. They are the size of a small pigeon, their bodies and wings a chartreuse green color, with a hooked nose on their Marilyn Monroe lipstick red heads. Originally natives of Peru and Ecuador, no one knows how they ended up in the city. The flocks are usually in the range of fifteen or twenty. At first they stuck to the Telegraph Hill area, but as the populations grew, they began spreading out. They've been spotted as far south as Sunnyvale.

"No. Relax," I said. "She just shoots into the air. The gun is empty, but the birds recognize the noise and take off."

I reached up for a sweet cherry and popped it in my mouth. "They were moving in on her cherries."

Gaby took off her hat and gazed up at the sky. "What do we do now? Wait and see what Logan and that creep Desi do next?"

"No. You don't wait on these kinds of characters. You stay aggressive. Come on, I'll walk you home and buy you lunch on the way."

We stopped at Mario's Bohemian Cigar Store Café on Columbus Avenue and split a meatball sandwich, then made our way to her house. There was no sign of Logan, Desi or anyone else who seemed to have an interest in Gaby.

She unlocked the door and invited me inside.

"Gaby, I'm afraid that I may need more money. I want to do some deep checking on Logan, Desi, Niven, and Gaucho."

"Why Gaucho?" she asked. "He's dead."

"Not if he called you from Argentina. What's his date of birth?"

"The tenth of June. I was never sure of the exact year."

She reached into the desk and took out the money-stuffed envelope and pushed it toward me.

"Not yet. Maybe I'll get lucky with some easy searches. But I am going to buy you a new answering machine with some of this money. You've got to start recording these anonymous calls and be ready in case Gaucho, or whoever is claiming to be him, calls."

"God, it's hell getting old. It's gotten so that I hate this electronic world we're living in: computers, smart phones, email, movie screen-size TVs, Twitter, whatever the hell that is. Everybody in a hurry. I liked the old days when we went to plays, intimate jazz joints, and took our time at talking, eating, reading a book and making love. Hell, they even have robots to take care of that now. Remember that old Broadway musical, *Stop the World I Want to Get Off?* Well, that's how I'm starting to feel."

"Stay safe," I told her. "And at any sign of trouble, give me a call."

She closed the door slowly, as if she was reluctant for me to leave.

I stood across the street and studied her house for a few minutes. It was hard to image that it was worth all of those millions of dollars—once torn down. It was in need of repair and it was vulnerable—to burglars, robbers, rapists, murders, and the likes of Desi. Entrance could be easily made through the front door or windows, the garage door, and the woods on east side of the property were an open invitation to climb into the backyard break in through the back. Nothing to stop the bad guys, except an elderly lady with a pistol, hunting rifle, golf club and a lot of pure grit.

CHAPTER 8

I started running checks on a website database that catered to private investigators. My favorite was inexpensive—the address check, just twenty-two dollars. I punched in Logan Carmichael's address in Redwood City and the information started streaming in. The check listed the name, sometimes date of birth, sometimes partial social security numbers, of anyone who had used that address on a credit card, bank loan, or retail credit account.

Logan took up a lot of space. He had filed for bankruptcy several times, the last three years ago. Paula was a co-filer on one of the bankruptcies. The first three numbers of her Social Security card were 680, which meant it was issued in Nevada. Logan's numbers were 449, which meant Texas. The information that was most helpful was on Desi Zuniga. A partial date of birth. A Gemini, May 22nd. No Social Security number.

There were no hits on Niven Carmichael.

I switched to a civil filings check on all three names. Logan was listed as a defendant in eleven different lawsuits: three in Los Angeles, three in Riverside County, two in San Mateo and three in San Francisco. Paula was named a codefendant in five of them, as was Niven Carmichael.

No filings under Zuniga's name.

I'd have to wait until tomorrow to run criminal checks on Gaucho, Logan, Niven and Desi from my source in the San Francisco Police Department, as well as my contact at the phone company. I wanted to check Gaby's landline number. There's always one thing you can count on from a private client—they won't tell you the truth. That alleged phone call from Gaucho was just too convenient.

If someone tries to disappear, they change their appearance, their IDs and their location, but one thing that they have real difficulty in changing is their habits.

I took a stroll down Columbus Street, stopping at a rundown storefront. The faded blue and white striped awning hung low enough to cause me to duck. The chipped tile entryway was missing a good number of tiles. The word Café on the window was nearly illegible.

All of this was done on purpose, to discourage customers. You had to wrestle with the accordion-grated gate to get to the weathered front door, and once inside, there were more problems. Four husky men, looking like they'd just gotten off of a freighter from an around the world voyage, unshaven and in need of haircuts, were sprawled in captain chairs, playing cards and smoking twisted ropes of cigars.

There was a bar of sorts—a thick plank of wood supported by sawhorses. Nano, the bartender, bore a marked resemblance to the great old character actor Mike Mazurki, he of the towering six-foot-five-inch frame and the craggy, intimidating face, who usually played a gangster or hit man in the hundred plus films he'd been in. I had little doubt that he was the "giant" that Gaby had seen in the Fior de

Italia doing business with Gaucho.

He spotted me and that craggy face broke into a wide smile.

"Nick. How are you? Do you want to see your uncle?"

"If he's available, Nano."

"For you he's always available."

He waved an arm wide and pointed toward the end of the bar. "You know the way and the right door."

There was a narrow hallway with two doors. The one on the left led to the betting room, which was filled with a bank of phones, piles of old-fashioned flash-paper that can be burned quickly, several computers and a few guys who went about the business of operating a gambling establishment. My Uncle Dominick, my father's only brother, is a bookie.

Nano must have sent a signal because the door swung open before I got there.

"Nicolo," Uncle Dominick said, wrapping his long arms around me and hugging me to his chest. "You look good." His right hand patted my head. "But the gray hairs, they are coming in, no?"

"More every day, Uncle."

His own head of thick hair was solid silver. He was a handsome man, still tall, with a straight back and broad shoulders that stretched the threads of his Broini blue wool suit.

I inhaled the familiar scent of Aqua Lavanda cologne, the scent that Dominick and my father had worn all of their lives. He ushered me into his office, which was filled with expensive leather chairs and polished walnut furniture. There were four big screen TVs on the walls, three were tuned to a different sporting event: football, baseball, basketball, and the fourth to a poker game.

His desk was cluttered with stacks of money in various heights, each held together by rubbed bands.

He poured us both a tot of crystal-clear Marolo grappa and waved me to a seat.

"How's business, Uncle?" I asked.

A shrug and an embarrassed smile. "I was thinking of retiring, but then the wise people in charge of politics decided to make sports betting legal, so now I'm busier than ever."

Uncle Dominick is known as being a Gentleman Bookie, meaning he didn't break the legs of those who reneged on their bets—he simply stopped taking their bets, the worst thing you can do to a gambler. He also dealt strictly in cash, which was why he had those characters hanging out in the bar. Nano was in charge of picking up losing bets and delivering money to the winners. Legalized gambling was fine, for those who didn't mind if the government knew of all of their transactions. Dominick's clients preferred to remain anonymous.

"I'm searching for someone who may have been a client of yours six or more years ago, Uncle. Ethan Carmichael. He disappeared. He went by the name Gaucho. His lady friend told me that someone who resembled Nano once did business with him in the Fior d' Italia."

Dominick leaned back in his chair and tugged at an earlobe, as if that would stir up his little gray cells.

He finally grinned and outlined a big mustache under his nose. "Yes. Gaucho. He was a good client. Reliable. Always paid off on time, until the end. When he disappeared he owed me, oh—" he bit down on his upper lip, "—something like three thousand dollars."

"His lady friend said she got a call from someone

identifying himself as Gaucho today. It could have come from Argentina. If so, and he is alive, I don't think he would have given up betting on the horses. Do you have any contacts down there?"

Dominick's forehead corduroyed. "Argentina? I'll have to think. I may know someone who knows someone. The Jockey Club in Buenos Ares is a very well-run operation. I'll make some calls."

"There were rumors that Gaucho owed a great deal of money to some Asian Las Vegas businessmen and that he may have tried to pay them off with a valuable painting."

"A Picasso float," my uncle said with a wintery smile.

"You're familiar with the term?"

"Oh, yes. Anyone in my line of business is. You become a pawn broker. Paintings, jewelry, anything of value, but especially wristwatches." He walked over to an antique Biedermier mahogany five-draw chest and pulled out the top drawer, revealing a treasure trove of watches and jewelry.

"When a client hasn't the money to pay off his loses, they will use whatever they have. I try to discourage that, but, that is the way it is."

He picked up a black-faced watch and offered it to me.

"A Rolex. Very popular in these transactions. The client can give it to me, and then buy a knockoff so that the wife, or the husband, will never know. Do you need a watch?"

"No thanks, Uncle." I didn't want the watch, but it did make me think about the Rolex Gaucho had left in his car the night he disappeared.

"Tell me more about the painting you were talking about, Nicolo."

"The artist is Ellsworth Kelly, it's titled Green on White 71."

"The name means nothing to me, but I will do some checking."

I thanked him, then stood up to leave.

He tapped his index finger on his chest. "Your health. You are well?"

"Very well."

The finger moved over and tapped one of the larger stacks of money. "And financially?"

"I'm fine."

He reached across the desk and cupped my hand in both of his.

"And Mrs. Damonte. How is she?"

"She is...the same, Uncle."

He squeezed my hand gently. "Nicolo. Sometimes 'the same' is very, very good."

CHAPTER 9

The next morning I slotted the Suzuki motorcycle in amongst a fleet of Harley Davidson solos in the back parking lot at the Hall of Justice.

I flashed my old inspector's badge at the bored uniformed officer checking people though the metal detector at the rear entrance. He gave me a quizzical glance, not recognizing me, but nodded his head in an okay.

It was becoming a mutual feeling. I'd been retired a good number of years now, and I didn't recognize many of the faces in uniform or plainclothes that roamed around the Hall.

Before taking the elevator, I found a nook by the stairway and made a call from my cell, which traveled all of four floors up to the Burglary Detail, in Room 414.

"Burglary Detail. How can I help you?" said the bright, always cheerful voice that belonged the detail secretary, Dolores Compos.

Dolores was one of those persons who always appeared to be happy, which couldn't have been all that easy for her. She was the mother of four: the hard way. Two sets of twins, all boys.

She was also the person who ran DMV and criminal

checks for me—for a fee. Those boys had to be fed.

I gave her the names, addresses and what ID I had on Logan, Niven, and Paula Carmichael, as well as Desi Zuniga.

"I need the works, Dolores." At the last moment, I provided her with Ethan "Gaucho" Carmichael's information.

There have been cases when people on the lam for a number of years got tripped up by simply getting a traffic tag.

"Dolores, who's the boss in Missing Persons now?"

"Lieutenant Jack Braun."

I heaved a sigh of relief. I knew Braun well enough to level with him.

I took the Hall elevator up to the fifth floor. It's always an adventure. They should sell tickets for tourists. Can't get out to Alcatraz Island? The Cable Cars are jammed? Fisherman's Wharf is too crowded, as is Chinatown and Golden Gate Park? Well, wait right here for the next elevator, folks. There will be a motley potpourri of bandaged victims: brassy-mouthed, low-cleavaged hookers, fidgety, nervous witnesses, and jurors on their way to court, as well as a couple of tired-eye plainclothes cops, and, last, and certainly least, a few well-dressed, briefcase clutching, noses-in-the-air attorneys who would much prefer to have an elevator designated for their use only. They don't mind representing the great unwashed, they just don't want to travel with them.

That morning's ride included the usual suspects, plus a well-dressed middle-aged woman in a multi-color patchwork fur coat who was holding a white, pink-eyed rabbit, complete with a red harness and leash, that she proudly claimed was her emotional support animal.

The Missing Persons Bureau had been expanded since my last visit there. Twice the size, two secretaries and dozens of cubicles.

Jack Braun came out to greet me. He was of medium height and trim build with fine blonde hair, thin on top and brushed tight against the side of his head.

"What's up, Nick?" he asked as he ushered me into his office.

It had been at least five years since I'd seen Braun and we did catch up for a few minutes, swapping lies and talking about mutual friends.

He poured us both a cup of coffee from a vintage Mr. Coffee machine.

"I hope you like it black," he said. "Now what's on your mind?"

"I was hoping to talk to whoever handled a case about seven years ago. A man by the name Ethan Carmichael parked his car by the Dolphin Club, and disappeared. It was assumed he went for a swim and never came back."

Braun cocked his head to one side. "What's your interest in the case?"

"Carmichael had a house on Greenwich Street. He was sharing it with a lady friend, Gabriella Maoret. It's kind of complicated, Jack."

I spelled out the details of the living estate, and the information about Ethan's brothers trying to pry her out of the house. "They really want her out of there. Maoret is my client. She hired me to...discourage them. That was on Saturday. On Sunday she told me she got a call from someone claiming to be Ethan Carmichael."

He cocked his head to the side again, and studied me for a few moments. I had the feeling he was trying to figure out just how much he could trust me.

"There's no blowback on you or the department on this, Jack. Carmichael was legally declared dead. The probate is closed. I'm just trying to help the lady."

Braun gave a quick nod, like a hiccup. "Gaby. The painter. I remember her. Nice woman. You're talking about Gaucho Carmichael. That's what everyone called him. I handled the case, Nick, before I got promoted to lieutenant. Did she think that the phone call was legit? That it was Gaucho?"

"She couldn't tell, said it was a lousy connection. My guess is that the brothers are screwing with her."

He took a sip of his coffee and winced. I didn't blame him. One thing that hadn't changed at the Hall was the lousy coffee.

"I'll tell you what little I remember, Nick. It was really a nothingburger. I mean, there wasn't anything there. This Gaucho was a member of the Dolphin Club. Swam in the bay a lot. He takes a final swim. Was it suicide? I was told his father committed suicide when he was a kid. You know the stats on that—a son is lot more likely to kill himself if his father did. Or was he just drunk? The body was never found, so, like I say nothing. Nothing but a lot of money involved, which put some pressure on me to dig a little deeper than the case warranted."

Another sip, another wince.

"The two brothers. I forget their names."

"Logan and Niven."

"Yeah, they were beauties. The younger one, Niven, floated the idea out that Logan had killed Gaucho. Then there was Gaucho's wife."

He pursed his lips together and let out a soft whistle.

"She was a real beauty, in more ways than one. A tough lady.

"And there were the attorneys. Everyone was well-heeled in the lawyer department, and the attorneys had some juice with the mayor and the chief. So I was getting some pressure, but to do what?" He shrugged his shoulders. "Unless Carmichael's body surfaced, there was not much to do. No body, no suicide note. A waste of the department's time."

He gave me a soft smile. "And I bet you feel you wasted your time talking to me."

I stood up and put my barely touched cup of coffee on his desk.

"No. I appreciate it, Jack. I owe you a lunch."

"Your client, Gaby. She really took it hard. The brothers and the wife were only interested in the money, but she was hurting. We shared a bottle of red wine. Best damn wine I ever had. She had a cellar full of the stuff."

"Not anymore," I said.

CHAPTER 10

I made a quick stop back at my flat, and went about finding Dan Forbes, the insurance investigator for Boston Fidelity that Gaby had spoken to. That wasn't much of a problem, the company's home office was in—where else? Los Angeles.

I caught Forbes at his office desk. He had been promoted to senior claims adjuster. He was quite cooperative once I explained the circumstances to him.

"I remember the lady, Gaby. She was really nice. I can't say that about the rest of them. They were a rough bunch."

"Was there much of a problem settling the claim, Mr. Forbes?"

"Of course we made a big issue over the possibility of suicide. That would have squashed the whole deal, but Ethan Carmichael didn't leave a suicide note. We went after the 'Dangerous Situation' clause in the policy, swimming the bay. But that didn't work. Many of the members of that club he belonged to all had insurance without that stipulation. Still, swimming out there at night was pretty dumb in my estimation."

"Did you deal directly with Ethan's brothers?"

"Oh, yes. Logan and Niven. They were a piece of work,

believe me. They brought in the lawyers and it was a real free-for-all. I did have a few meetings with Ethan's wife, Rhonda I think it was."

Forbes blew a stream of air into the phone. "From what I recall, the brothers settled with her a year or so after Carmichael had disappeared. She got a house in southern California and some paintings, then promptly divorced Gaucho and married some other lucky guy.

"Boston Fidelity not only had a life insurance policy on Mr. Carmichael, we had his business end too, which brought the claims up to close to three million dollars, so I spent quite a bit of time on the matter. Are the two brothers still alive?"

"They are."

"They didn't much like each other back then."

"It's worse now, Mr. Forbes."

He laughed lightly, then said, "Be sure and say hello to Miss Gaby for me. I really liked her. Is she in good health?"

"She's hanging in there."

"Well, if somehow Mr. Carmichael's remains surface, we'd like to know about it. I've always felt that there was something fishy about the whole matter."

I called my source at the phone company for the records on Gaby's phone, and then went out shopping, stopping at the Walgreens on Polk Street and paid all of $24.33 for an answering machine.

Gaby was at home, appearing nervous and slightly tipsy. I installed the answering machine and spent an hour with her, going over the photographs on the walls, as well as her paintings.

I'm no art expert, but her works seemed to have a special quality about them. Someone once told me that you can tell a really good painting by observing the brush strokes. "Was the artist in charge of the brush, or the brush in charge of the artist?"

Gaby's canvases signaled that she was in charge.

I was in neutral gear until I received the criminal, DMV and phone records, so I decided to take a stroll down to the scene of the crime.

A cool northern wind had scalloped the grayish bay waters and lowered the temperature, but not the enthusiasm of the tourists who were enjoying themselves at Fisherman's Wharf, on foot or riding a two-wheeler rented from the Blazing Saddles Bike Rentals.

The line at the cable car turnaround near the Buena Vista Café stretched out to Aquatic Park, almost down to Jefferson Street, where Gaucho had parked his car in front of the Dolphin Club the night he disappeared.

The club building is a two-story batten board building with blue trim around the porthole-style windows and deck.

The gray-sand beach alongside the club had a group of shivering men, women and children staring at four men dressed only in swim trunks, swim caps and goggles, who had just come out of the frigid bay water. They weren't shivering, but their skin did have a bluish tint.

They were laughing at something. One of the men yanked off his goggles, shook the water from his hair and started roughly patting his legs and chest with the palms of his hands.

"You're going to hurt yourself, John," I called out.

He gave me a measured stare and then broke out in a grin.

"Lord of mercy, it's Nick Polo himself."

My long-ago radio car partner John Lynch lumbered

over toward me. He was in his sixties, and thick through the chest, stomach and shoulders. He had bowed legs and walked in that sailor's side-to-side style that Vladimir Putin used, as if he'd just gotten on shore after a long voyage.

When John offered his hand, I made sure that mine went in all the way up to the webbing between his thumb and forefinger. He had one of those bone-crushing grips, which he used to discourage the pickpockets who preyed on tourists around Market and Powell Streets.

"Still working as a private eye, Nick?"

"Still at it. I have a case involving a former club member who disappeared a few years ago."

I pointed to the fire hydrant a few yards away. "Parked his car right there and supposedly took his last swim. A man by the name of—"

"Gaucho Carmichael. Yeah, I knew him. Interesting guy. We got pretty friendly. Really generous. I hit him up for a donation to the PAL, and the man wrote out a check for ten thousand bucks."

The PAL, Police Athletic League, is a volunteer organization that helps local kids, getting them into football, baseball, jiu-jitsu, and taking them on fishing trips.

John started windmilling his arms and jogging in place.

"He wrote me two checks like that. I believe that he was murdered, Nick. I used to swim with him a lot. He always timed his swims, every link of it, on is watch. A blue-faced Rolex Daytona. He loved that watch. It had three little stopwatch dials on it. A, what the hell do you call it?"

"A chronograph."

"Yeah. He loved showing it off. He told me he paid over twenty-three thousand dollars for it. I told him he was crazy. No watch is worth that much money. He had an answer.

The guy always had an answer. Said it would only cost $6.47 a day if he wore it every day for ten years."

Someone had recently paid seventeen-point-eight million dollars for Paul Newman's Rolex Daytona. I wondered what that would add up to per day for ten years.

"He left the watch in his car, along with his wallet and clothes, John."

"I know. But if he did come down here for a late-night swim, he'd have worn the watch. And there was no towel or robe in his car. You come down here for a swim, and the club is closed, you have a towel and robe close by."

"Maybe not, if he was going for a final swim."

"Suicide? There are easier ways to do it, Nick. You just don't get tired in the water and sink to the bottom. There's a lot of pain involved—those last gasping breaths, you can't stop from gulping for them, and you're sucking in saltwater, gagging. Pure agony."

He pointed to the Golden Gate Bridge, some two miles to the west. The bridge was in full postcard picture mode: the twin towers poking out of the thick bank of fog rolling in from the Pacific Ocean.

"That's the way to do it, pal. Hop over the railing and they say you've got time to say an act of contrition before you hit the water, and when you hit, it's all over."

John squeegeed some water from his hair. "He was killed somewhere else, his stuff left here."

"There's a theory that he may have just taken off. He was having money trouble."

"Could be," John conceded. "But he would have taken the watch with him."

"When was the last time you saw Gaucho?"

"Jeez, I don't know. A week, maybe more before he

disappeared."

"Can you remember how he was? His mood? What he talked about?"

"Horses, I think. He'd liked to talk about horses. It was a long time ago, but I kind of remember the club had a swim, and everyone went inside for a few drinks. Gaucho was pretty handy with a Scotch bottle and he wasn't shy about buying a round for the house. More than that I can't tell you, Nick. I'll ask around, talk to the other members, but truth be told, I don't think it will do you much good."

I got home and had just enough time to finish a glass of Chianti before Mrs. Damonte came knocking on my door with her hands full. She was carrying a fresh-from-the-oven *Torte Della Nona*—Grandmother's cake, a delicate crust with silky pastry cream covered with fresh cherries from the backyard tree.

She headed right for the kitchen, placed the cake on the table and then whipped out deck of Tresette cards, an Italian card game that's a little like gin rummy.

"What was your impression of Gaby Maoret," I asked her as she scanned the kitchen for dust or dirt.

"*Lei ha un carico problematico.*" She has a troubled soul.

I explained that Gaby had suffered through a terrible illness.

"*Il suo corpo è ancora debole e la sua anima è molto scura.*" Her body was still weak and her soul is very dark. She went on to say that Gaby had two very good guardian spirits protecting her, and that in a previous life she had been a famous French courtesan who had dated nobleman and a certain pope.

Mrs. D had given me one of her soul readings years ago. I have two guardian spirits, Yvonne and Raul, the problem is that they are both *molto pigro*, very lazy. I'd also had lived two earlier lives: one as a Benedictine monk, at their monastery in Subiaco, Italy in 564 AD, and another as a blood thirsty 19th century Italian pirate who plundered the Gulf of Mexico.

She had no explanation as to what my soul was doing between those two gigs.

It was interesting how all of her soul readings came up with such interesting past lives; never just a chambermaid, a plumber or a tailor.

I told Mrs. D that she and Gaby seemed to get along well, and perhaps that was because they were from the same part of Italy.

No, she protested. Gaby was from Sanremo on the Riviera, where everyone was rich, and they had a church with twelve steeples and a grand casino.

While I was sampling the cake and Mrs. D was shuffling the cards the phone rang.

It was Gaby.

"Can you get over here right away? There's a man at the door who says he's Niven Carmichael. He scared the hell out of me. He looks like Gaucho now. He wants to talk, and he has a suitcase. Can you come?"

"Is he trying to force his way in?"

"No. I told him I was calling someone and he said he'd wait."

"Five minutes, Gaby."

I may have been off by a minute or two when I pulled the Polomobile right up to Gaby's stairs. A man was sitting next to the door, his legs dangling down the steps.

He made no move to get up as I climbed the stairs. He was wearing a black leather jacket, faded jeans and scuffed desert boots. His long curly gray hair was tied back with a rubber band. He had a long nose, on which perched a pair of horn-rimmed glasses and his mustache pretty much matched the ones I'd seen in the pictures of Gaucho Carmichael.

He took his time as he climbed to his feet.

"Hi," he said. "I'm betting that you are Nick Polo."

"Did Gaby give you my name?"

"No. My brother Logan did. I'm Pastor Niven Carmichael."

He hoisted up his canvas camouflage print duffel bag and said, "Can we go inside now?"

"When did you talk to your brother?" I asked.

Niven put the bag down between his feet. "Earlier today. I'm afraid Logan doesn't like you. And Desi. He *really* doesn't like you at all. Now, can we go inside? I'm thirsty, have to go to the bathroom, and would like to talk to Gabriella."

"First I'm going to pat you down."

Niven's whole body stiffened. "For a weapon? I don't carry weapons."

"Then you won't mind if I make sure."

He held his hands up over his head like a soldier surrendering to the enemy. That's when I noticed his wristwatch.

I gave him a thorough check and learned that he was telling the truth. No weapons. I also learned that he was a long time between baths.

"Okay, Gaby. Open up."

She opened the door slowly, inch by inch.

Niven reached for his duffle bag and I told him, "Let's leave it here for now. It'll be safe."

He started to protest. His glasses fell off and he caught them in mid-fall.

"This is ridiculous," he huffed, as he edged his way into the house.

Gaby was wearing an over-sized black cardigan sweater. Her right hand was in the sweater's pocket and I had a hunch it was wrapped around her pistol.

"We met some time ago, Ms. Maoret," Niven said, with a slight bow from the waist. "It's a pleasure to see you again."

"What do you want?" Gaby asked bluntly.

"For now, permission to use your restroom and a glass of water. With ice please. It's been a long day."

She pointed, with her left hand. "Down that hall. Second door on the left."

"I don't like this," she said when Niven was out of sight.

"Let's hear him out. And you can put your gun away. He's not armed. Get him some water. And maybe a glass of wine for us. I've had a long day too."

She returned with a tray and three glasses, two stemmed ones with red wine, and a tumbler loaded with ice at about the same time Niven came back from the bathroom.

He thanked her profusely and drained the water in three long gulps.

"Now what do you want?" Gaby repeated, her lips barely moving.

"Perhaps I should explain myself, and tell you what I've been doing lately."

"Go ahead," I said, jumping in before Gaby could bark at him.

Niven settled down on a chair and started speaking in a back of-the-throat manner, his chin pointed upwards as if he was giving a sermon.

"I've just returned from Peru. This very morning. I've been living there for more than a year, in the Andres Highlands, helping the natives. The very poor natives. You can't believe the poverty. I'm working on building houses. They live in shacks, cardboard boxes, or filthy caves now. The new houses will be six hundred square feet. Quite small by our standards, but they will be like mansions to them."

He squirmed in the chair for a bit, while Gaby and I stood sipping our wine.

"The problem of course is money. It takes money to build these houses. I'm trying to obtain enough funds to purchase an industrial 3D printer. That would cut the construction costs in half."

"They make 3D printers for houses?" Gaby asked skeptically.

"Oh, yes. They're huge. Concrete and water are pumped through the printer and it slowly lays out a foundation and then the walls. It's the coming thing."

More concrete. The Carmichael brothers seemed obsessed with it.

Niven coughed into his fist before continuing. "My church is working—"

"Your church?" from Gaby. No skepticism this time, pure sarcasm.

Niven was unfazed. "Yes. I've found God. I'm the pastor at The Church of All Lands. We're really making a difference."

He rattled the ice in the bottom of his glass, indicating he'd like a refill. Gaby ignored him.

"Just exactly why are you here, now, Pastor?" I asked.

"Well, to find funding for my church. I know Miss

Maoret is entitled to live here as long as she wants. I was hoping that we could come to some kind of an agreement. One that she would be happy with and would allow for the sale of the property. The money I would receive would go directly to the church. And the people. Especially the children." He opened his eyes wider and raised his eyebrows. "It would save a great many lives."

"Humph," Gaby said, snorting through her nose.

"Gaucho told me that he had purchased a valuable painting just before he disappeared. Has it ever turned up? Could he have hidden it somewhere in this house? That would really be helpful for the church."

"There is no painting," Gaby said.

Niven wasn't giving up. "Like I said, I just arrived here today, and I have nowhere to go. I was hoping that I could stay here, in the house. I don't take up much room, and I would be happy to do anything. I've become quite competent as a carpenter, plumber, whatever you needed, Ms. Maoret. And we could talk about just what is best for you."

"Your brother Logan has already talked to me enough," Gaby said. "I don't want you here, and I'm staying put until God or the devil comes and gets me."

Niven placed his hands on his thighs and pushed himself to his feet. "I'm sorry you feel that way." He turned his attention to me.

"I have very little money. Could you suggest a place to stay?"

"You could always hock your watch. Is that Gaucho's on your left wrist?"

He pulled the sleeve of his jacket back a few inches and smiled shyly. "Yes. It's all I have left from Gaucho. I'm prepared to sell it to help the church when the time comes."

"Let me see that," Gaby said.

Niven unclasped the blue-faced Rolex and handed it to her. She held it close to her eyes and examined it like a jeweler.

She grinned and passed it to me. "It's Gaucho's all right. Check the inscription."

There were just three words: *I'm worth it.*

I gave him back the watch. "Niven, go out and wait for me by my car. I'll take you to a place for the night."

He made a final weepy-eyed plea to Gaby, then he left.

When he had closed the door behind him I asked Gaby, "What did you think of him?"

"I trust him about as much as I trust gas station sushi. Church, starving children, he's full of it."

She was gulping in big breaths of air and her face was deeply flushed.

"I'm hungry, Gaby. What say I drop Niven off somewhere, then come back and pick you up and we have dinner at The Stinking Rose?"

That cheered her up and she agreed quickly. The Rose is just a few blocks from the house and was famous for the amount of garlic used in their dishes.

Niven was leaning against my car. I told him to put his duffel bag in the backseat.

When he had his seatbelt in place, I turned over the engine.

"Why the fancy mustache, Niven?"

"I always admired Gaucho's." He wiped his hand across his face. "I get a lot of compliments."

"You really don't have a place to stay?"

"No."

"Why won't your brother put you up?"

"There's certainly plenty of room, with just the three of them living there, Logan, Paula, and Desi. Not even a cat or a dog, just those sharks in the aquarium. I had hoped that Logan had changed, that he would be a little more reasonable, but he still carries his hatred for me. Money can do that to people."

"We're talking about a lot of money. Both of you burned through millions."

I turned west on Union Street, as Niven explained where the money went.

"Business dealings, with the wrong people. You'd be amazed at how fast the money can disappear."

"Someone called Gaby yesterday, claiming to be Gaucho. She said it sounded like him, but she couldn't be sure."

That got his attention. He straightened up, his head almost hitting the headliner. "Gaucho? What did he say?"

"That he was sorry about leaving, that he wanted to come back. Gaby said that the connection was very bad, but she could hear someone in the background speaking Spanish. Argentina-styled Spanish."

"That's impossible. Someone was playing a joke. A bad joke."

I hooked a left on Polk Street, then turned east on Bush and pulled up to the curb in front of the four-story Regency-style red brick building that housed the Music City Hostel.

"This is a neat, clean place that's also pretty cheap. Have you got enough money to get you through the night?"

"Umm, I'm, quite low until I can get to a bank tomorrow."

I dug one of Gaby's hundred-dollar bills from my wallet and dropped it on his lap. "Do you have a cellphone?"

"Yes." He wrote the number down on the back of a Starbucks receipt.

"What do you think happened to Gaucho, Niven?"

He smoothed out the hundred between his fingers. "I think he took his own life. He was quite edgy at the time, there were business problems and his ex-wife was hounding him something terrible. He was drinking, doing drugs. He...we, over the years often talked about suicide. Our father did just that when we were very young. Something like that stays with you, Mr. Polo. He had this fascination with guns, as did our father. I'm surprised he didn't do what Dad did. Dig his own grave and then blow his brains out."

"Why did your father kill himself?" I asked.

"I was so young. Gaucho said that he had lost all of his money, and that he was very sick."

Niven ran his hand over his face and worked his jaw.

"I have few memories of my father, but what I do remember is that he was very nice to us, always bringing home presents, taking us fishing and hunting for rabbits. It hit all three of us very hard. I have to give a lot of credit to Gaucho. He held us together. At least in the beginning."

He exited the car, pulled his duffel bag out of the back and then placed his left hand on the car's roof and leaned down so that we were at eye level.

"Thank you for the money. I'll pay you back, and I want to warn you again about my brother, but especially Desi. He really is upset. He kept telling me he was going to get even with you."

"Keep in touch," I said as I pulled away into traffic.

CHAPTER 11

Dinner with Gaby at The Stinking Rose went well. After her third glass of red wine she started telling some wild tales of her time with Gaucho as they traveled the world and the fun she and her sister had growing up in Sanremo.

I walked her to her front door, she was a little wobbly, and made sure she locked it once in the house.

Mrs. Damonte was standing at her front door as I trudged up the steps to my flat. She was dressed up in full battle gear. The pockets of her dragging hem-on-the-ground apron (black of course) were stuffed with spray cans: Raid, mosquito spray, ant spray, wasp-freeze spray and WD-40, all good defense weapons. In her right hand was her trusty BB gun.

"*Qual è il problema*?" I asked. What's the problem?

She responded is such rapid Italian that I had to ask her to slow down.

A man had come by, knocked on her door. A fat man with *capelli come una scopa*, hair like a broom.

She patted her hip. And he had a pistol. Silver, like the Lone Ranger.

"What did he want?" I asked her.

"*Tu. Parla inglewse, poi spagnolo, vuole sapere se vivi qui.*"

He wanted me. He spoke Spanish and English, loud and slow. Spanish and Italian have some similarities, so she was able to understand some of what he had said.

Mrs. D pounded the butt of her BB rifle on the cement. "*Ti ha chiamato mio nipoti*!" He called you my grandson. She didn't like that at all.

She then pinched her ample chin between her thumb and forefinger. He'd pinched her chin and said that he would be back to see me.

"*Si pizzicava forte e faceva male.*"

He pinched hard, and it hurt.

And the man had left a package for me. It was now in her kitchen sink.

Her kitchen usually smells of roasted meats, herbs, spices, fresh bread and cookies, but now the strong scent of old fish dominated the room.

The package was wrapped in newspaper. I picked it up cautiously. If was soft, spongy, and there was no doubt of its contents. I unwrapped it and rolled out a slimy, gray-green colored lingcod.

Lingcod are common in the Bay Area and can be caught anywhere from the rocks off Alcatraz to the Farallon Islands and up and down the coast. They can go up to eighty pounds, and have a very large mouth and eighteen sharp teeth.

This one was about ten pounds, and stuck between those sharp teeth was a business card. My card. The one I'd handed to Logan Carmichael at his place in Redwood City.

Of all the many varieties of rock fish, the ling was my

favorite, as well as of many restaurants' chefs. Delicious. But this one was going right into the garbage.

"The man's name is Desi, and he in very bad. Do not answer the door for him again. He actually hurt you?"

"*Si, madre stronza!*"

The "MF" word. She was really mad.

"Don't worry," I said. "I'll take care of him."

There was no mystery as to how Desi had found my address. While it wasn't listed on my card, anyone with access to a real estate database could pull it up through assessor records.

Desi was mad at me, and wanted to prove how tough he was, and I didn't doubt that he was damn tough, but hurting Mrs. D. That was enough to make a Sicilian's blood boil.

I got to work on Desi early the next morning.

The California DMV and criminal check information on Logan, Niven, Paula Carmichael and Desi Zuniga were sitting in the tray of my fax machine, as was the phone record for Gaby's landline.

The only one with a criminal record was Logan: three drunk driving charges in the last five years.

Paula was clean, not even a speeding ticket.

As was Desi, but his driver's license was issued just fourteen months earlier. The DMV addresses for all three was the house in Redwood City. The Lincoln Continental was registered to Logan and Paula Carmichael, the Escalade to Desi Zuniga, again, all at the Redwood City address.

No criminal record for Desi in California, and no mention of his having applied for a concealed weapons permit.

Checking his criminal record in Mexico would be costly, and the records are unreliable. Pay the right people the right money and records vanish.

There was a story recently regarding the Mexico military confiscating the guns of every single member of the Acapulco Police Department. The reason? Corruption via the local drug lords. The story didn't spell out whether the cops were doing the corruption or that the military was.

Niven was a washout. His California DMV license had expired six years ago. The listed address was in Los Angeles. It did have one detail of interest: his full date of birth, which would help with further checks.

Gaby's phone records were mostly local and up and down the peninsula, except for one international number that she called just once: 00-39-334-977-7037.

I ran the number through the web. It belonged to someone in Sanremo, Italy, Gaby's hometown.

My index finger hovered over the phone. Call the number? Or not? I chose not.

The trouble with a case like this, working for a private client without a great deal of money, is that it limits your access to the really good background checks.

I could have easily burned through Gaby's entire three thousand dollars plus in digging into FBI and Interpol records, passport records, and detailed credit information, all illegal of course, thus expensive.

That's why you should never get entangled with the feds, no matter what agency: FBI, CIA, or the whole alphabet soup of departments. Some of their agents may not be all that bright, but they have access to everything, and all of the money they need to make your life miserable.

While on the web I checked on the Church of All

Lands, supposedly Pastor Logan Carmichael's church in Peru. Nothing of record. I did find that the San Andres Highlands area was indeed filled with a great many poor people. It was also known as cocaine valley.

In many occupations it's not *wha*t you know, it's *who* you know. Being a private investigator, you have to know a lot of people who are either on the borderline, or the opposite side of the law.

Khatia Navana is one such person that I deal with whenever I need some electronic help. We all have our pluses and minuses, and tech expertise is something I'm definitely lacking.

Khatia is a lovely, dark-haired, voluptuous Russian woman in her thirties. She goes by the name Khat, and her storefront shop is located on the corner of 11th and Clement Streets, in the city's Richmond District, which was once a Russian stronghold. Now Clement Street is often called the city's second Chinatown, due to the number of Chinese restaurants.

The shop's windows were dusty, spider-webbed and filled with a hodge-podge of batteries, soldering tools, computer parts, wire cutters, transistors and lots of little things with wires sticking out on one end of which I had no idea of what they were.

A video surveillance camera greeted me with a blinking red light as soon as I entered the shop.

Hip-high boxes of all shapes and sizes formed a labyrinth, a zig-zag path that led to a counter jammed with several computers and one large brass Victorian cash register with exposed, typewriter-like keys and a hand crank that looked as if it would have been at home at the Long Branch Saloon in Dodge City.

Khatia was alone, leaning over, her elbows on the countertop. She had long strings of corkscrew curls that flew in front of her face when she shook her beautiful head.

Her clientele included hobbyists, computer programmers, surveillance specialists, security agencies, guys who eventually sold things that they claimed had fallen off a truck, and in-need private investigators.

"Nick. Long time no see. Whatcha need?"

"Help, as usual. I want to set off the car alarm on a certain Cadillac Escalade."

"That's it?" she said with a disappointed pout. "When are you going to bring me a real challenge? Have you got the exact year and VIN-number of the car?"

"I've got the DMV printout right here."

Khatia scanned the printout, nodding her head, sending her hair dancing.

"Umm, umm, umm. Easy money." She grinned and handed me the printout back. "But quite a bit of easy money."

"How much?"

"Three hundred for the alarm alert. If you want to pop the door and trunk locks, it'll be double, and if you want to start the engine, tack on another hundred."

"Just the alarm. When can I have it?"

"There's a Starbucks down the street. By the time you come back with a cinnamon raisin bagel and a pumpkin spice frappuccino, it'll be ready."

Khatia was true to her word. When I got back from Starbucks she had a black plastic box the size of a matchbook waiting for me. It had a white button in the center.

"Click the button once and the horn will go on, Nick. Click it again and the horns turns off. There's only one caveat. If there are other Cadillac Escalades within twenty yards of the one you're interested in, they may go off too."

"That shouldn't be a problem," I assured her. "I need one more thing, a throwaway phone."

"I sell a lot of those, Nick." She pointed a finger at a display of small burner, disposable cell phones. "How many calls are you thinking of making."

"Just one."

She slipped one of the phones from the display rack. "Then this is your baby. Twenty-five bucks. I'll activate it for you."

When I got back home I checked with Mrs. D. No one had been by.

I asked her, "How would you like to have some guests for dinner tonight? Gaby, and maybe one more person."

"*Chi*?" Who?

"It could be one of Uncle Dominick's men."

At the mention of Dominick she seemed to blush, and one of her little feet pawed at the floor. My uncle was the one and only member of the Polo family that could do no wrong in Mrs. D's eyes.

She got back to normal quickly, and rubbed her thumb a forefinger together, the universal signal for she wanted some money.

"*Dovrò comprare qualcosa di buono.*"

She would have to do some shopping.

Then I called Gaby. I told her that I wanted her to make a phone call later in the afternoon, to Logan Carmichael.

She wasn't happy about that.

"Just call him, and say that you want to meet with him and Paula, but definitely not Desi."

"I don't want to meet with them," she protested.

"You won't. I'm not sure of the time yet. But when they come, you'll be here having dinner with Mrs. Damonte."

She still wasn't too happy.

"It's important, Gaby. Trust me."

"Okay," she said. "Can I bring something?"

"Wine."

"All right. And I'll bring a picture of Gaucho for Ludovica. One I took myself. She thinks it may help her read his soul."

"I'll call you back in a little while."

My next call was to Uncle Dominick.

"Ah, Nicolo. I was about to contact you. I had friends in Buenos Aires check up on your Gaucho. He is not known at the track or with any of the prominent bookmakers there."

"Thank you, Uncle. Another favor. I was wondering if Nano would be available to stay at my flat this evening for a few hours. Someone made a threat at me, and Mrs. Damonte. I'm going to take care of it, but I want someone with her tonight."

"Mrs. Damonte? I'll come myself."

"You're always welcome, but if you come, Mrs. D might never let you go. I think Nano is the right man for what I have in mind."

"So be it," Uncle said. "Let me know if you need more help."

I prowled around the basement for burglar tools and found what I needed: a heavy-duty wire cutter, a roll of black Gorilla tape, a five-pound First Alert home fire extinguisher, and a can of red spray paint. I had a two-foot-long section of one-inch rubber coated copper wire in the trunk of my car that worked well as a sap.

I had no time to shop for a balaclava, so I pressed Mrs. D into cutting out eyes and mouth openings in an old navy watch cap.

That was, I hoped, all I would need.

I called Gaby and told her to contact Logan Carmichael.

"Remember, you want to meet with Logan and Paula. If Desi is anywhere in the area, the meeting is off. Make it for eight o'clock."

She hemmed and hawed, but finally agreed. She called me back in minutes.

"It's set. Logan was curious. I just told him it was time for us to meet again."

"Good. A man will pick you up at six o'clock. You'll recognize him. He was the giant who met with Gaucho at the restaurant. He works for my uncle, who is a bookie. He'll walk you to my place and you and he can enjoy Mrs. Damonte's dinner. I'll be back around ten o'clock. Okay?"

"Where are you going?"

"We'll talk about it when I get back."

I broke the connection before she could ask any more questions, then called my uncle and passed on the instructions for Nano.

So now all I could do was wait until the sun started to go down.

CHAPTER 12

I arrived at Logan's house in Redwood City around five o'clock and found a good surveillance spot a half block away under a gnarled maple tree with roots that had buckled the street and sidewalk. Everything depended on Logan and Paula leaving together, and Desi staying in place.

The Lincoln and the Escalade were parked around the side of house, but sitting directly in front was a chocolate brown Audi sedan.

At five twenty-two the front door opened and Paula Carmichael escorted an attractive woman over to the Audi. She was Kaye Palmer, the Realtor.

They shook hands in a friendly manner, then Kaye drove off, through the opened fence gate. It stayed open, which was a good sign.

I sat back, nibbled on the fried anchovy-stuffed zucchini blossoms that Mrs. D had supplied and wondered what Kaye was up too. Getting Gaby out of the house obviously, but Gaby hadn't mentioned anything about a Realtor contacting her. Kaye was getting her ducks in a row: get the Carmichaels to agree to an offer that she could present to Gaby. I couldn't blame her for trying.

The sun had gone down, the night was motionless and

clear. I could smell a charcoal BBQ nearby.

At six-thirty, Logan, Paula, and Desi exited the house and strolled over to the Lincoln. Paula was wearing a light blue pantsuit, Logan a tan leather jacket and 49ers cap. Desi was in a black T-shirt and jeans, his holstered revolver at his hip. If he got into the Lincoln, I was screwed. But he stayed back, letting Paula open and close the driver's side door by herself, while Logan slipped into the passenger seat. Maybe those drunk driving charges kept him from getting behind the wheel.

Desi thumped the Lincoln's roof with his hand as it drove off, through the still open gate. He retreated back into the house, and the gate stayed open, which meant I wouldn't need the wire cutter.

It got very dark, very fast. The moon was a well-honed cycle, and necklaces of vehicle lights sparkled along the freeway.

It was showtime. I put on a pair of tan leather golf gloves, gathered up the Gorilla tape, copper wire sap, paint spray and the fire extinguisher and walked up to Carmichael's front gate. Still open. The gods were with me. So far.

I entered the property and sank down in a nest of shadows, took the electrical gadget that Katina had made for me and pushed the little white button.

Right on cue, the Escalade's horn emitted a loud, steady beep-beep sound.

Within a minute Desi burst out of the front door, hand on his pistol grip, his head whipping around.

The house's outdoor lights were not as bright as I had expected, which was all to the good.

Desi strode over to the Cadillac. I could hear him

swearing in Spanish. When he reached for the car's door, I pushed the white button and the beeping stopped.

He seemed puzzled as he walked around the car, his big hands pulling at the door handles.

Then he patted the car's hood, as if he was calming down a horse, and headed back into the house.

I pulled down the balaclava and moved in closer. There was loud music, the Gypsy Kings performing "Bomboleo," one of their best.

The lone cactus plant gave me enough cover, so I pushed the alarm button again.

Desi had a bottle of beer in his right hand this time.

When he was out of sight I slipped in the front door. More Gypsy Kings music. No sign of another person. I switched off the alarm button and waited behind the open front door.

I could hear Desi coming, swearing, his boots pounding on the cement flooring.

As he passed by I said, "Boo."

He swiveled his head around and I blasted him right in the face with the foam from the fire extinguisher.

He dropped the beer bottle, slammed his hands into his face and screamed. I gave him more of the foam, then went to work with the sap, starting on his right shoulder, then as he continued to rub his foam-covered face, I kicked him hard between the legs. He bent over in pain, giving me a perfect target—the back of his neck.

He slumped to his knees. Another neck shot and he went all the way down, and out.

I tugged the revolver from his holster and then checked his vitals. He was breathing erratically and blowing foam from his mouth.

I made a quick check of the area. No one else. Just Desi, me, and the Gypsy Kings.

I got a towel from the kitchen, wiped down his face, then went to work with the Gorilla tape, binding his hands behind his back, taping his mouth shut, then a final piece of tape over his eyes.

I helped myself to a beer from the refrigerator, then picked up a wooden kitchen chair and carried it down the steps and into the sunken room with the aquarium.

The lights were on. The sharks weren't in sight.

I positioned the chair in the middle of the floor, and then came the hard part—dragging Desi over to the chair.

He was half-awake, mumbling, trembling, his legs starting to come to life, kicking wildly.

I pressed the barrel of his revolver against his forehead and said, "*Cállate*!" Shut up.

Even with a face full of fire extinguisher foam, a possible broken shoulder, a neck that must have hurt like hell, and eyes and mouth taped shut, the impression of a gun barrel is unmistakable.

I got him to his feet and pushed and shoved him in the direction of the aquarium room. He stumbled on the steps and fell to the carpet. More pushing and shoving until I got him into the chair. Then I tapped his feet together, his arms to the back of the chair. The tape job wasn't perfect. Desi was a big, strong hombre, and once he was fully awake it would probably take him a half an hour or so to get free—unless the sharks somehow got to him.

I went back to the kitchen and finished my beer. The boom box playing the Gypsy King music was sitting right in the middle of the kitchen table. I cranked the volume up to full blast.

Desi was wiggling in the chair, in danger of toppling over. I ripped off the tape covering his eyes. More mumbling blinking and head shaking.

I gave him a minute and then let him get a look at me. All he saw was the balaclava and his gun in my right hand.

When I was certain that his vision was all right, I pinched the flesh under his chin very hard, then slowly pointed the revolver at the center of the aquarium tank and fired all six bullets.

Water streamed through the bullet holes for a few seconds then the glass cracked open wide and the water poured into the room.

I jumped back and climbed the steps to the hallway.

The water rose up to Desi's ankles.

I didn't see the sharks. There was still some water in the bottom of the tank. I felt sorry for them, but they were due to be butchered in a couple of days, so maybe this was a better way for them to go.

Desi must have chewed through the tape on his mouth, because he was now screaming at the top of his lungs.

While the Gypsy Kings were blasting out "Volare" I used the spray paint can to graffiti some of the walls with *Regla de Los Zetos* statements—Los Zetos Rules, the drug lord gang that Logan and Desi had tangled with in Mexico.

A final look at Desi, still in the chair, still screaming, and then I put the revolver next to the boom box, picked up my gear and hurried back to my car.

I used the throwaway phone for a call to 9-1-1. In a bad imitation of Marlon Brando playing a Mexican revolutionary in *Viva Zapata* I mumbled, "Hurry. 713 Bay Road, Redwood City. Gunshots. I think it's a gang fight. Hurry."

* * *

There was a mixed bag waiting for me in Mrs. Damonte's flat when I got back home.

Mrs. D, Gaby, and Nano were sitting at her kitchen table, playing cards. Each had a number of poker chips in front of them: Gaby's had the most, Nano was a close second, and Mrs. D was way down.

Gaby, grinning, giggling, one hand clasped around a tall highball glass filled almost to the top with red wine. Nano had an amused smile on his craggy face, and Mrs. D appeared to be……pissed off.

They were speaking Italian, Gaby saying something about the price of veal at the Little City Market on Columbus Avenue.

She turned her head when she saw me and switched to English.

"Nick. How did it go? Is everything all right?"

"I'll know more tomorrow. Nano, thanks for your help, you can take off if you want."

He started to stand up, then Mrs. D gave him sitting orders: He was too far ahead. She wanted a chance to get even.

"*Trattare e giocare,*" she told Gaby. Deal and play.

They were playing *Trieste,* Mrs. D's favorite. It's played with just forty cards: no queens, tens, nines or eights.

Gaby dealt, she bet, she won the hand.

"*Ancora uno!*" Mrs. D demanded. One more deal.

Gaby did just that, and won again, picking up all of Mrs. D's chips.

I don't know how much they were playing for, but Mrs. D is not used to losing, probably because she plays mostly with me, and I let her get away with cheating. She was eyeing Gaby's quickly depleting wine glass as if she'd like to pour some Pine Sol into it.

Gaby took no notice. She was back to Italian, singing and laughing while Nano counted the chips and replaced them with dollar bills and quarters.

While Gaby was sliding her winnings into her purse, Nano said, "Nick, I can walk her home. I'll make sure she gets into the house and that no one is hanging around. If there's anything that doesn't look right, I'll call you."

I readily agreed. If Logan or Paula Carmichael were still waiting at the house, one look at Nano as her protector would send them on their way.

"I'll stop by in a little while," I told Gaby. "I want to talk to you."

She got busy passing out hugs and kisses to everyone and thanking Mrs. D for the wonderful dinner.

When they were gone, Mrs. D gave me her evil eye look and stomped back into her kitchen.

"*Lei imbroglio!*" She cheats!

"Nano won some money too," I told her.

"*Eera solo fortunato.*" He was just lucky.

The remains from dinner were cooling on the stove: veal involtini with prosciutto and parmesan. I took a bite. Even cold it was delicious.

Mrs. D may have her faults, but not feeding the hungry is not one of them. She warmed a plate and I helped myself to the left-over wine.

"Did you examine the photograph of Gaby's friend Gaucho?" I asked.

She walked over to the cabinets and drew a black and white photo from a cutlery drawer.

It showed Gaucho with a smirk on his face, a cigarette dangling from his lips.

She placed it very near her eyes and then laid it gently on the kitchen table.

"*Un uomo misterioso.*" A mystery man.

According to her reading Gaucho had a sudden change in his life. All of his good fortune had vanished. Of course she could have picked up all of this from her conversations with Gaby.

"Did he kill himself?" I asked.

She upped her performance by scratching at the photo with her fingernails, as if she could scrape away the mystery.

"*Un uomo misterioso, ma aveva paura.*"

He wanted to leave this world, but he was afraid.

"Of what?"

"*Morte. Il diavolo.*" Death and the devil.

"It is believed that he drowned himself, here in San Francisco Bay."

"*Non acqua.*" Not water.

"Then what?"

She picked the photo up again and began massaging it with her thumbs. She would need more time. More photographs.

"How would you like to have Gaby stay here, with you for a day or two?" I asked her in Italian.

Her first response wasn't encouraging.

"She is a nice lady, and is in danger."

Mrs. D calmed down a little, but needed more encouragement.

"You could have nice talks, and play cards. You could get even with your winnings. Probably make some money. She won't be able to cheat, once you've seen her play a few times."

"*Senz'altro!*" she said. Basic translation—damn right.

The winds had calmed down and the night was mild. I debated briefly. Walk the six blocks or take the motorcycle. I decided on the bike but was feeling lazy and left the helmet in the garage.

Nano was hovering around Gaby's front entrance when I parked the Suzuki in her driveway.

"I thought I'd wait for you, Nick. No one's around. She's inside." He grabbed my elbow and leaned over and whispered, "The lady is crocked. You want me to stick around a while?"

"No, we're good. Thanks Nano. I may need you again."

He tugged down the brim of his pinch crown wool fedora that would have looked good on Bogart, except that size-wise it would have probably fallen down to Bogie's shoulders.

Gaby was indeed crocked, but she seemed happier than I'd seen her before—the wrinkles smoothed out, the frown lines in retreat, her eyes on full sparkle.

"Damn that woman can cook," she said, holding her skirt above her knees and going into a full, if unsteady, pirouette.

"She can indeed. Have you checked your phone, Gaby?"

"No. Was I expecting a call?"

"I have a hunch that Logan or Paula may have left a message."

The answering machine was blinking—the call count number was on five.

"How about I check the messages while you make some coffee?"

"Coffee? I don' want no stinkin' coffee," she said in an exaggerated deep voice.

We were back in Bogart land, *The Treasure of the Sierra Madre*, with no stinkin' badges.

"I could use a cup," I said. "I'm going to call Logan and I don't want him to know that you're here with me."

She stumbled a bit and held onto a chair for support.

"Where'd you go tonight, while we were all eating veal and playing cards?"

"I was right here, outside, watching Logan and Paula wait for you. How about the coffee?"

A hiccup and a burp, and then she said, "You'll have to drink it all yourself," before tottering off toward the kitchen.

I ran through the five recorded calls, all in Paula's voice. They started out politely, but ended up rude and vulgar: "Where the hell are you? We've been waiting for an hour."

I called the Carmichael number and got Paula's voice again. She still didn't sound happy.

"This is Nick Polo."

"Who?"

There was all kind of chatter and movement in the background.

"Nick Polo. The insurance investigator. I wanted to explain to you why Ms. Maoret wasn't there to greet you at her house tonight."

"Where was the bitch?"

"She had a heart attack. I took her to the hospital."

Paula's voice lowered and smoothed out. "Oh, that's too bad. Is she dead?"

"No. It was a very mild attack. She's fine."

Disappointment pulsed through the phone line. "Well, we've all got problems. A group of four Mexican punks, armed with guns, broke into our place, shot it up, and beat the shit out of Desi."

"Four of them?"

"Three of them held him down while the other one sprayed him with a fire extinguisher and beat him with a rubber hose."

Desi upped the count. It would have been tough on his ego if he reported that he'd been overpowered by a single intruder, "Is he all right?"

"I don't know. He went to the emergency hospital. We've got cops all over the place. The Mexicans spray painted their goddamn gang slogans all over the walls and then shot out the aquarium glass, with that useless Desi's own gun. I told Logan he was worthless in Mexico. He's no better here!"

"That's terrible. Did the sharks survive?"

"Sharks! Who cares about the sharks? This is going to cost us a fortune!"

"Paula, I saw Niven earlier. You should get in touch with him. He needs help."

"Niven? He probably brought those goddamn Mexicans here with him. And tell that old bitch I want her out of our house!"

Gaby brought me my coffee. She had a coffee cup too, but hers was filled with red wine.

She yawned widely and said, "I think I'm going to bed."

With Desi out of operation and Paula and Logan involved with the police, there didn't seem to be any danger in leaving Gaby alone for the night.

We said our goodbyes and I was climbing onto the Suzuki's seat when there was the roar of another motorcycle coming up Greenwich Street. It was a big metallic-blue bike with gold-colored spoke wheels. It did a skidding U-turn and ended up right in front of Gaby's stairs. The driver, wearing a black leather jacket and an orange-colored full-face helmet, pulled something out of his jacket. I could see the muzzle flashes and hear the unmistakable high-pitched cracks as bullets slammed into the stairs and ricocheted over my head.

Five shots in all, then the motorcycle roared off.

Gaby opened the front door and shouted, "What the hell was that?"

"Are you okay?"

"Yes, but—"

"Lock the door and call the police."

Lights from the neighboring apartments began to pop on as I hit the ignition, pulled the choke out all the way and shot out onto the street.

I could see the taillights of the big bike speeding straight down Greenwich. When it reached Stockton Street it had to slow for a fire department engine returning from a run. I sped down the hill, swerving to miss a young couple too engrossed with each other to bother about traffic.

The driver of the big bike looked back in my direction, turned south on Stockton Street, then made a looping right hand turn on Filbert, skimming by the customers who had edged into the street while waiting to get into Mama's Restaurant.

He zoomed past St. Peter's and Paul's Church and right through the yellow light at Columbus Avenue.

I had to jockey my way through the red light to get after him. He continued south on Columbus, accelerating sharply to get through the green light at Broadway, a main thoroughfare. There was a chorus of beeping horns and strands of pedestrians were waving arms and shouting curses as I shot through the intersection just as the signal changed to red.

I was gaining ground. He was driving a touring bike, either a Harley or a BMW, big, powerful as hell, virtually a motorbike built for two, but not nearly as fast or as nimble as my Suzuki.

It was as if he was riding a Clydesdale and I was on a thoroughbred.

Riding a motorcycle is all about the lean angles you take when turning or maneuverings through traffic. I was getting the impression that the guy wasn't that skilled a driver. His turns were wide, cautious, awkward looking.

It wasn't exactly a *Bullitt*-style chase. No flying into the air and landing on the pavement in a thud, no burning of rubber, and no stunt drivers or cops directing traffic for the shoot.

It had been a long time since I'd been involved in high speed chase and I was feeling that familiar combination of exhilaration, fear and excitement as I goosed the Suzuki's engine.

A sergeant on the SFPD solo unit described it as feeling like a quarterback in the last seconds of a close game. Somehow your brain takes over and focuses your attention where it needs to go. Parts of the street and buildings were just blurs, but as I edged up closer I could make out the bike's high windshield, the twin aluminum luggage cases, the upturned collar of the drivers leather jacket, the distinctive BWM emblem, and the license plate: black and white—Texas, with a lone star.

The driver took his right hand from the handlebar and was groping around inside his jacket.

He'd fired five shots at Gaby's steps. There are a few guns that carry just five bullets. Very few, and there are a lot of semi-automatics that have seventeen cartridges in the magazine.

Shooting at someone from a moving motorcycle is for the movies and TV screens only, unless you're crazy. And I had no reason not to think that this guy was crazy.

I dropped back and sure enough, he pulled out a gun, only to wave it over his head to gain some leverage and throw it toward the sidewalk just before he made a right turn on Washington Street, avoiding a man in a red jacket who moved out of the way with all of the grace of a matador.

We were in the heart of Chinatown now and street speed slowed down to five and ten miles an hour as we both wove our way through cars, LimeBikes, and Segway scooters. It was easy to keep track of him with that orange helmet.

At times we both came to complete stops while red lanterns swayed in the breeze and the soft yellow glow from the 1920s' streetlamps competed with the bright neon glows from dive bars and restaurants.

I was worried that the driver would simply abandon the motorcycle and vanish into the islands of onlookers flooding the sidewalks.

I was also worried about getting too close. He'd thrown a gun away, but there a strong possibility that he had another one at the ready.

The big bike's power paid off when he turned left and barreled straight for the Stockton Street Tunnel, a thousand-foot tunnel that runs under a side of Nob Hill.

Motorcycles can accelerate much faster than most cars. Roll back the throttle and a good bike can reach one hundred mph in just a handful of seconds. That's fast enough in a car, but on a bike it feels twice as intense.

I felt the wind in my face as I closed in on him.

The roars from our engines echoed off the tunnel's red and yellow tile walls.

The BMW took a wide, wavery turn, going west on Sutter Street. A muni bus was hogging both lanes and he leaned on his horn button as he careened around the bus.

I was able to cut the corner and move up to within thirty yards of him.

He tried some fishtail moves which only allowed me to get in closer. He sped up again, rocketing through the Powell Street intersection, avoiding a cable car, but almost skidding out of control while side-slipping on the tracks.

He seemed to have the bike under control again as he made a right turn on Taylor Street.

The 900 block of Taylor is often featured in movies and TV series. Bordered by the Masonic Auditorium on one side, and the Huntington Hotel on the other, the incline is so steep there are steps built into both sides of the sidewalk.

It is also one of the three steep hills that the SDPD uses for motorcycle training purposes. To graduate to full driver duty, you have to speed almost to the top of the street, at California, and then make a one-hundred-eighty-degree turn. During that turn your lean angle is about twenty degrees and it feels as if you're just inches from the asphalt.

The bike with the shooter was now chugging up the hill, with me just a few yards behind him.

Then he made a bad mistake; he slammed on the brakes and tried to make an abrupt left turn at the same time. You can't do that with a motorcycle. There was a loud screeching noise and the driver catapulted over the front fender, his head taking full impact as the bike threw him into a streetlight.

I managed to avoid the tumbling, out of control bike

and pull to a bucking stop on the sidewalk steps.

The driver still had his helmet on. Blood was streaming down the side of his face and his body was laid out in a tortuous position, his right arm twisted backward at the elbow, one leg stretched out at an upward angle that even a yoga master couldn't achieve.

I knelt beside him. He was alive, making soft gurgling sounds, spewing out more blood.

I had no intention of removing his helmet, that would be a job for a skilled paramedic, and there was no need to try and lever up the face mask. The blue-faced Rolex chronograph on is left wrist was all the ID I needed.

The BMW motorcycle had been reported stolen by Raymond and Joyce Pickett, from Marble Falls, Texas. They were in the midst of a cross-country trip when they ran into a man who identified himself as Niven Davis at the Music City Hostel. Niven had bought them dinner and drinks, but when they woke up the next morning, their motorcycle, along with the husband's orange-colored helmet, were missing.

The gun Niven had used to fire at Gaby's staircase, with me in the all-too-close vicinity, was never found. Someone had picked it up after he'd thrown it to the street and decided to keep it.

Niven was taken by ambulance to the Zuckerberg San Francisco Emergency Hospital and Trauma Center on Potrero Street. It's the city's largest primary care facility and the only Level 1 Trauma Center within thirty miles.

I stopped by to see him the following morning. The hospital staff was busy, efficient and full of energy: nurses and doctors moving along at top speed, patients on gurneys being wheeled to operating rooms.

There was that distinctive smell of alcohol, cleaning agents, and an airborne scent of fear and sickness.

Niven Carmichael was covered in more bandages than the Invisible Man in those old movies. He was lying prone on a single bed, his left leg and left arm in plaster casts, his neck in a halo brace cast. He had a full head wrap with just an opening for his eyes and mouth and tubes were slotted in both nostrils. A medical monitor was beeping out numbers and squiggling lines next to the bed.

Niven was asleep, or out under the pain medication he'd been given.

I stared down at him feeling uneasy, partially blaming myself for his condition. Should I have just let him go? I had seen the BMW's license plate. If I'd just given that information to the police, they would have traced the motorcycle to him.

The shots he'd fired weren't aimed at me, I was sure he hadn't even seen me sitting on my bike in the driveway on Greenwich Street. They were warning shots to scare Gaby.

You can't look at someone in his condition without wondering what was in store for his future. Will he walk again? Be paralyzed? The way Niven had impacted with that streetlight, some form of brain damage was a real possibility.

A nurse in a green uniform, a surgical mask in place, her honey-blond hair done up in a tight bun, brushed past me.

"Are you a relative?" she asked.

"No."

"Out, please."

I backed out into the hallway and watched her go

through her tasks. First, washing of the hands in the sink. Dry hands. Put on purple latex disposable gloves. Examine patient. Adjust bandages on Niven's face. Check medical monitor and tubing. Gloves into the garbage, another hand washing in the sink.

The nuns at the Catholic grammar school I attended pounded into us, literally at times, that the proper length of time used in washing your hands consisted of saying a Hail Mary while you were applying that soap and water.

At the rate that doctors and nurses wash their hands now a days, they must get in two or three full rosaries a day.

A slim, dark-haired woman with nutmeg-colored skin approached me.

She had a clipboard in hand. The plastic ID tag pinned on her starched white blouse identified her as Terry Hansen, Financial Counselor.

"Good morning," she said. "Are you a relative of Mr. Carmichael?"

"No, but I think I can help you out. He has been living out of the country, in South America for some time. I do know that he has a brother, Logan Carmichael, living here in the Bay Area. How's his condition?"

"Complicated," she said warily. "We are having difficulty in getting background information on Mr. Carmichael. The only identification he had on his person when the ambulance brought him in was his passport."

"I don't believe his brother knows about Niven's accident. I'm driving down to see him now."

"Then you're a friend."

"Not really." I gave her one of my cards. "It's complicated."

She slipped one of her business cards from the clipboard

and handed it to me.

"Please have the brother contact me as soon as possible. I need much more information regarding the patient."

I promised her I'd do just that.

Things were busy at Logan's house in Redwood City. There was a uniformed security officer at the entrance gate and several construction trucks spread around. The perimeter fence was in the process of being replaced, and Logan and Paula were jawing with a man in bib overalls and a spanner in one hand.

Paula looked like she'd just left the makeup table, and was wearing another pair of tight shorts and a red halter top. Logan was in a rumpled battleship-gray polo shirt and had a pair of sunglasses hanging from a cord around his neck.

"Halt right there," the pot-bellied security guard said sternly.

I halted, showed him my badge. "Logan's expecting me."

He dragged the gate back and I drove in, parking alongside a sky-blue PG&E utility truck.

Paula spotted me and hurried over.

"Is she still alive?"

"Gabriela Maoret? Yes, she's fine. But someone else is not. Logan's brother Niven is in critical shape. We better have a talk with Logan."

Logan wasn't too happy about that. The house was in a turmoil so we sat in the Lincoln, with all four doors wide open, Paula and me in the backseat, Logan up front.

I gave them a condensed version of what had taken place, leaving my part in the motorcycle chase out entirely.

"Why the hell would Niven do something stupid like that?" Logan demanded. "Shooting at the house. How do you know it was him?"

"I saw him. Five shots."

I passed Terry Hansen's business card to Logan. "This lady is the hospital's financial counselor. She wants to talk to you."

Logan frowned as he read the card. "I'm not paying for any of this. Niven wasn't working for me, he's on his own."

"He's close to dying," I said. "And if he survives, he's going to need a lot of medical care."

"He's on his own," Logan repeated, banging a hand on the dashboard.

"Niven has a half interest in the house on Greenwich Street," I said.

Paula curled her legs up on the leather seat. "Where did you hear that?"

"Out of the corner of my ear."

Logan began playing with the sun visor, pushing it up and down.

"All right. I'll give her a call."

He climbed out of the Lincoln, stretched his head to the sky and let out a mournful bellow, so loud that it startled some of the men working on the fence.

"Why me? Why me? These goddamn Mexican terrorists and now my brother fucks me!"

I helped Paula out of the backseat. She tottered on her high heels and held onto my arm.

"What happened to Desi?" I asked. "I don't see him around."

"You won't!" Logan said angrily. "That incompetent bastard is gone for good. I never should have brought him up here."

"I told you that," Paula said ever so sweetly. "Many times, dear."

Logan kicked out at the Lincoln's front tire, forgetting that he was only wearing a pair of flip flops. It definitely wasn't his day.

CHAPTER 13

Things stayed somewhat quiet for the next few days. I got to working on some new cases for old, valued clients.

I visited the hospital to see Niven Carmichael again. The prognosis wasn't good—there was a strong possibility that Niven would end up being a quadriplegic.

No one deserves that.

Then a package in the mail came for me. From Gaby. Inside was the gold and blue abstract painting of hers that I had admired, and a handwritten note:

> Dear Nick:
>
> IT has come back. I'm going to a cancer clinic in Tijuana for treatment. There are some new alternative therapy programs that sound promising. What the hell have I got to lose? Just my life, I guess.
>
> I have made a settlement with Logan Carmichael on the house. It will be turned over to him, and Niven, I guess, in three months, just enough time for me to have all of my stuff cleaned out of there.
>
> The paperwork was handled by a lady Realtor, Kay Palmer. Nice gal, says she knows you.
>
> Use the attached key to check things out if you

want. Most of the paintings will go to the art institute, but if there's one that interests you, be my guest. Same goes for the photos. Giving all of that up really hurts!

Sincere thanks for all your help, and if I beat IT again, we'll really have a celebration!

Best,

Gaby

P.S. Say goodbye to Ludovica.

A house key was taped to the back of the letter.

I wandered over to Greenwich Street. The key slipped easily into the lock. The key wasn't really necessary. The tumbler pins were so loose I could have opened it with a pair of paper clips.

Gaby had moved out in a hurry. At least a third of the photos and paintings had been removed from the walls, most of them left learning against chairs and couches, or just lying flat on the floor.

I rummaged through the photographs and picked up one of Gaucho that appeared to be fairly recent. He was frowning into the camera lens, looking like he wished he was somewhere else.

The pearl handled revolver was missing from the bureau drawer.

The kitchen was mostly intact. I checked the refrigerator. There was a half-full bottle of Dry Creek Fume Blanc chilling nicely on the top shelf. It seemed like a shame to waste it, so I poured myself a glass and then took a quick tour of the rest of the house, finding little of real interest. Her closets and bedroom bureaus were full of upscale label clothing. There was no sign of her safari jacket, the putter, or the hunting rifle she'd mentioned. The other rooms on the second floor were filled with sealed cardboard boxes and dusty furniture.

The art gallery on the third floor looked much the same as it had on my last visit. That left the basement. The same three cars were parked in the same spots as last time.

I checked the wine cellar. One big change there. The door of the dark green Cary iron floor safe was wide open. Gaby had told me she didn't have the combination, didn't need it, because she had nothing to put in there.

I was washing out the wineglass in the sink when I heard the front door open.

"Hello? Anyone home?" a cheery voice shouted out.

It was Kaye Palmer. She was dressed in shades of brown again, including a Gucci suede over-the-shoulder tote bag that screamed out to muggers: Take me! Even if there's nothing inside, I'm worth over three thousand bucks!

She didn't seem surprised to see me.

"Miss Maoret told me she'd given you a key, Nick. I hope you're not mad that I brokered a settlement between her and the Carmichaels."

"Not a bit, Kaye. But I would like to know the details."

She dimpled her cheeks. "Well, since you're responsible for getting me started on this, I think we should discuss it at lunch."

Kaye never did tell me just how big her piece of the pie was on the deal, but it was big enough not to cause her to even blink when the waiter at Mr. Jiu's, on Waverly Place, presented her with the check for our roasted squab and bottle of Arnot Roberts Chardonnay.

Gaby Maoret got her half a million dollars, in the form of a cashier's check.

Logan could start demolition and then construction in ninety days. Gaby was happy about the deal. Logan was happy. And Kaye was happy. I should have been happy after downing most of that ninety-dollar bottle of wine, but the open safe in the wine cellar had me wondering—what had Gaby kept in there?

Sicilian lightning broke out shortly after three the following morning. I could hear the sirens, a few at first and then the added choruses that signify a major alarm fire in underway.

A peek out my bedroom window confirmed my suspicions, smoke and flame coming from the vicinity of Coit Tower.

By the time I got to Gaby's place it was fully engulfed in the fire. A half dozen fire rigs had squeezed into the cul de sac. Fire hoses, like strands of spaghetti, were strewn all over the street.

One fire truck had its one-hundred-foot telescopic ladder extended up high enough so that the lone firefighter manning the Gorter nozzle-tipped three-inch hose could direct the stream down onto the house's roof.

There's a feeling of organized chaos at a big fire, with the firefighters and their apparatus moving in different directions. It seemed obvious that Gaby's house would be totally destroyed, and the department's main concern was now to keep the fire from spreading to neighboring structures and the forest leading up to Coit Tower.

The fire chief always wears a white helmet. I found him barking orders into a handheld radio. He gave me a withering "get out of my face" glance, then I flashed my badge and said, "Chief, Nick Polo. I was in the house yesterday. There are no residents, human or animal."

"Thanks. Stick around and talk to the Arson guys."

I did just that, watching the dangerous part where the firefighters were actually fighting the fire, and then the tedious, and still dangerous job of mopping up, with the wet charcoal stink of the smoldering embers thick in the air.

It was almost six o'clock when most of the trucks and engines were sent back to their firehouses. The house's roof had collapsed, but the walls were still up. The garage door had burned away and I could see that all three of the cars Gaby was renting space to were goners——charred out hunks of metal, their tires melted flat to the ground.

"Hey Nick," a voice called out. "Long time no see."

The firefighter removed his helmet and I recognized Tim Riordan from the Arson Squad.

"The Chief tells me you know something about the house."

"I do, Tim." I glanced at my watch. "Why don't we talk about if over a cup of coffee?"

Riordan swiveled his head around. "The coffee wagon didn't show up."

"It's after six. Gino and Carlo's is open now."

The bartender at Gino's wasn't surprised to see a firefighter in a dirty turnout jacket saddle up to the bar and when I nodded and ordered two coffees he topped off both cups with a shot of Jack Daniel's.

Riordan was a big husky Irishman with a mop of prematurely gray hair.

He took an appreciate sip of his drink and then said,

"What have you got for me, Nick?"

I gave him the full story, which carried us through another drink, then Riordan said, "No doubt it's was arson. Whoever started the fire wasn't trying to hide it. There were several ignition points on all three floors. Streamers, sheets and blankets, were rolled out throughout the house, dosed with what I bet the lab will determine was gasoline. A lot of the windows were wide open to provide more oxygen for the fire. I'm not sure yet, but there were a number of wax deposits, probably from candles. There's a professional arson gang that specializes in that. They buy cheap drug store candles, impossible to trace. They burn at about a rate of one inch every forty-six minutes, giving the bastards plenty of time to get away from the scene. You think this guy Logan Carmichael would have hired a pro gang for this?"

"Tim, I think that if he tried to start the fire himself, he would have burned himself up in the house."

"Then I'm going to have to have a long talk with him."

"Talk to his wife Paula too," I advised him. "She's the brains and the beauty of the outfit."

CHAPTER 14

Gaby Maoret hadn't left a forwarding address with Kaye Palmer, or anyone else.

There were a number of cancer clinics listed in and around Tijuana, but none of them would confirm that Gaby was a resident patient.

I was in my kitchen about to make a breakfast omelet when Mrs. Damonte rang the bell. She waddled in, full of energy, saying that she had been getting signs from the spirits about Gaucho Carmichael.

She took over the omelet chores while I went to the office and dug around for Gaucho's photograph that I'd taken from Gaby's house before the fire.

A simple omelet: eggs, butter, salt, pepper, a slice of French bread fried in the pan. I make it, it's fuel for the body. Mrs. D does and it's somehow a gourmet meal.

While I wolfed down the omelet, she examined the photograph, giving it the full up-the-face treatment.

"*Si. Era già malato.*" Yes, he was very sick.

Then she went into handwringing charade about Gaucho's spirit. It had been close, but it has moved. Far away now.

"Where?"

She needed more time. And more photographs.

I asked her if the spirits had told how Gaucho died.

"*Dolcemente. Nessun dolore.*" Softly. No pain.

Niven Carmichael was still alive, but in a great deal of pain.

Logan and Paula had been interviewed by Tim Riordan, but no evidence was found that connected them to the arson fire, which gave them full clearance to start the demolition of the house.

Gaby was still a no show.

Eight days later, things started to get interesting. I received an email, and then a phone call from Laura Feveral, my lady friend who was studying painting in Paris. She still loved me, wanted to see me, but couldn't leave Paris for another month. Would I fly over for a week or so?

"Please, Nick. I really miss you," she said as if she meant it. "I'll pay for the flight."

Laura was somewhere between well off and filthy rich, and I didn't hold that against her, but I told her I'd try and be there within the week, but that the flight was on me.

She started spinning exciting tales of where we'd go and what we'd do in beautiful Paris.

Twenty minutes later the phone rang again. It was Uncle Dominick.

"Nicolo. Are you still interested in the painting by Mr. Ellsworth Kelly? The green on white one?"

I'd forgotten all about the painting. "Yes, Uncle. You have news?"

"It has changed hands. Not a Picasso Float. A straight cash transaction. The figure I was given was seven hundred thousand American dollars."

"Do you have any information on the seller or buyer?"

"The seller was a private party, Nicolo. The buyer a collector from Las Vegas who prefers to remain anonymous. I'm told that if sold at auction, the price could have perhaps been double."

Gaby disappears, the house burns down and then the supposedly missing painting is sold. That was some trifecta, but then it got better, or worse.

Human remains were discovered during the demolition of the property on Greenwich Street. They had been buried in the backyard, under the cement pad with the golf mat, right where Gaby told me Gaucho had planned to put in a hot tub.

The body had been covered with dirt and then cement.

Positive identification was obtained through dental records. The remains belonged to Ethan Gaucho Carmichael. Initially Logan was gratified that the mystery of his brother's death had finally been solved, but then he began receiving calls from the Boston Fidelity Insurance Company.

That's when Logan and Paula asked for a meeting with me.

"It will be worth your while," Paula promised.

The meeting was set for the second-floor cafeteria of the Zuckerberg San Francisco General Hospital.

Just before I was ready to leave the flat, the phone rang. It was the call I'd been dreading. Lieutenant Larry Braun of the Missing Persons Bureau.

"Nick. What the hell is going on? Where is Gaby Maoret?"

"I honestly don't know, Larry."

"Jesus! What's with her? There I was, sitting on her back deck, drinking red wine, feeling sorry for her, and just fifteen feet away Gaucho Carmichael was taking a dirt nap."

"Gaby sent me a letter, just before the fire, saying that her cancer problem had returned and that she was going to a clinic in Tijuana for treatment."

"You believe that?"

"I don't know, but I don't think she had anything to do with the fire."

"Then who? Gaucho's brother, Logan? He's been calling me, asking me to get after Gaby, claiming that she must have killed his brother."

"Have you seen the autopsy?"

"Yeah. He was just put in the ground, no coffin, no embalming solutions, so the body deteriorated quickly. No trace of organs remained. Just bones and teeth. There were no traumatic wounds, no evidence of a bullet wound, nor any rope or duct tape that could have been used to bind him.

"The coroner found two empty bottles of 1989 Haut Brion Bordeaux lying next to the body. No glasses. Maybe he chugalugged them."

"What's the department planning to do?"

Braun's voice turned frosty. "Damned if I know. The guys in Homicide don't want nothing to do with the case, since there's no actual sign of a murder, and working a case from seven years back is a real pain in the ass. I guess it all depends on what the D.A. determines.

"Maoret certainly is the number one suspect. Hell, maybe she just got him drunk, dropped him in the hole and covered him up. That parking his car by the Dolphin Club and leaving his clothes and Rolex on the front seat was a nasty piece of work. Damn her to hell. She made me look like an awful dummy."

"I know the feeling, Larry."

"Oh, there's another guy who is been bugging me. Dan Forbes, an insurance investigator. I remember talking to him years ago. He was pushing for an investigation to show that Gaucho committed suicide. And Nick, you don't owe me a lunch anymore, it's going to be a dinner, at Morton's Steak House."

The hospital cafeteria was a clean, sterile affair, with a mix of some forty people: doctors, hospital staff, and dour-faced visitors. Like most hospital cafeterias, you're better off just sticking to a cup of coffee. Hidden speakers spewed out gloomy elevator music of the type that if you were in the elevator you'd push the stop button and take the stairs the rest of the way.

Paula had that crisp just out of the shower look: hair in perfect order, smelling of something expensive. She was wearing a white ankle-length leather coat and matching purse. Logan's hair looked like it had been attacked by a sparrow searching for nesting material. His jeans were bunched around his ankles and his company-logoed sweatshirt was in need of a wash.

I'd been at a table waiting for them for nearly fifteen minutes. Paula apologized, saying that they were visiting Niven.

"How's he doing?" I asked.

"Not good," Logan said. "But that's not what we want to talk to you about, Polo."

"It's Gaby," Paula said. "Gabriela Maoret. We have to find her. Actually, we want you to find her, and we will be happy to pay you for your time."

Logan picked up a packet of sugar and shook it up and down. "You were tight with her, Polo. You probably know where she is right now."

"Dear, could you get me a cup of coffee?" Paula said. "And maybe a donut or something sweet."

He pushed himself to his feet and said, "Don't give away the store while I'm gone," before heading to the food counter.

"Nick, we really have to find Gaby. The discovery of Ethan's body presents us with a serious problem. The insurance company now says that evidence suggests that he committed suicide. We've seen the autopsy report and there is no evidence of that, but they're making all kinds of legal threats."

She went into a long tirade about how rotten and unethical Boston Fidelity was.

Logan came back with a tray holding two cups of coffee and two pieces of lemon meringue pie.

"So what did you tell Polo," he asked as he passed out the coffee and pie.

"Just that we want him to work for us."

"What if I found Gaby? What do you want me to do?"

"You should arrest the damn woman," was Logan's idea. "There's no doubt that she killed my brother. Hell, he couldn't have covered himself up with that cement. And the goddamn cops are too lazy to go out and find the bitch."

"Now Logan, let's not jump to conclusions. Here's what I think probably happened, Nick. Gaucho passed away, naturally. Perhaps he had a heart attack, or he slipped and fell, an accident that killed him."

"So why would Gaby bury him in the backyard?" I asked.

"For the money. She was greedy," was Logan's theory. "Gaucho probably had a lot of dough on him, and there was that painting that still hasn't turned up. And she figured that with him gone, she was going to get kicked out of the house. She'd have to start paying rent like everyone else does."

Paula attacked her pie, finishing it all up in five big bites, while Logan skimmed the meringue off slowly and licked his spoon.

"Well, will you do it for us, Nick? Find her?" Paula asked.

"I'm still betting he knows where she is right now," Logan said.

Paula unlatched her purse and drew out a manila envelope.

"Find her, Nick. Get her to sign this affidavit, which states that Gaucho simply passed away, that there was no suicide. If you do that, we'll play you fifteen thousand dollars."

Paula shoved the envelope across the table. "Can you do it? Can you find her?"

"I can try. Oh, by the way, the arson squad has a lead on who started the fire. Some professional gang that has been working up and down the state."

That fib almost caused Paula to cough up her pie.

I stopped at the fifth floor to visit Niven Carmichael. There didn't seem to be any change in his condition, nor was there for the guilt that I had for being responsible for his injuries.

I found Terry Hanson, the hospital's financial counselor, in her office on the main floor. She thanked me for putting her in touch with Logan.

"He's been cooperative, but his brother's long-term medical situation is going to be a problem."

A man in his mid-thirties wearing a putty-colored Burberry trench coat, complete with epaulets on the shoulders, was leaning on the front fender of a white Buick Regal sedan parked in front of my flats. I nosed the Suzuki into the driveway, then went over to meet with him.

He had dark brown, lost beagle eyes. Golf cufflinks peeked out of his sleeves. "Dan Forbes, I presume," I said as I held out my hand.

"How'd you figure that out?" he responded with a smile.

"You match the description that Gaby Maoret gave me, and I heard that you've been digging around."

"Yes. Trying to locate Ms. Maoret. We're very anxious to talk to her. Let me get something."

He opened the Buick's front door and came out with a black leather attaché briefcase, then used the car's hood as a desk as be began thumbing through folders and envelopes.

"You don't mind doing business on the street, do you Mr. Polo? I've got a meeting with the medical examiner in less than an hour."

"What do you expect to get from the medical examiner?"

"We want our own expert DNA people to examine Mr. Carmichael's remains. His brother is rushing to get them cremated."

That was a good idea from the insurance company's point of view. There are autopsies and there are autopsies. The city's M.E. does a very good job, but. There's always a but. Sometimes they are really busy, the work has to get done, but unintentionally, out of necessity, corners are cut.

Then there are the DNA tests. There are a lot of toxicology labs in the Bay Area, some are better than others, some are more expensive than others.

If the deceased is a public figure, a politician, or the case involved is in the headlines and on TV every night, then everything goes first class. But the seven-year-old remains of an unknown male doesn't get that kind of attention, unless it's from an insurance carrier trying to recover a few million dollars.

Forbes pulled a paper from the briefcase and waved it in front of my face.

"This is a contract from Boston Fidelity, Mr. Polo. We want you to help us find Ms. Maoret. The contract stipulates that you are entitled to a three percent finder's fee, on the first million dollars recovered from the Ethan Carmichael estate, if information provided by Ms. Maoret helps us in recovering said monies."

His eyes bounced up to mine. "Three percent of a million is thirty thousand dollars."

"Technically Gaby's still my client."

Forbes snapped the briefcase shut. "Technically she's a murderer."

"You don't know that for a fact."

"Exactly. And I don't believe it. I spent some time with her. She's a sweet, caring woman. I believe that she assisted Mr. Carmichael in committing suicide, at his request. Just as his father did, and in the same manner, in a backyard grave."

"His father shot himself."

"True. We've yet to determine what killed Mr. Carmichael, but we will. And we want Ms. Maoret's assistance in proving that, and we are more than willing to provide her with excellent legal assistance should she need it. You knew her, worked for her. She must have given some clue as to where she might go."

"Gaby did tell me that she had health issues. Cancer. It had been in remission for years, but it came back. She talked about going to a clinic for help."

That perked Forbes up. He almost clicked his heels.

"When? Where?"

"A few of days ago in a letter. She didn't mention where. Finances wouldn't be a problem. She received a settlement from Logan Carmichael in the amount of a half million dollars just before she left."

Forbes popped open the briefcase again, grabbed a notepad and started scribbling.

"A half a million? For what?"

"Giving up her lifetime estate agreement on the house on Greenwich Street."

"And this had to be just before the fire."

"Yep."

Back to the briefcase for a business card. "Find her for me. There will be a bonus in it for you. A big bonus."

CHAPTER 15

I had an idea as to where Gaby took off to, so it was time to lean on my uncle again.

"You say she received a half a million for leaving the house, and you think she was the seller of the Kelly painting. That's a total of one million, two hundred thousand. It's really not a lot of money anymore, Nicolo."

There was probably a couple of hundred thousand stacked up on his desk. "It's a tidy sum, Uncle. She is in her mid-seventies and is not in the best of health."

"She is intelligent?"

"Very. And gutsy."

"So she planned this well. It was not just a sudden decision."

"I believe so."

"Some of the money should stay in cash, the other could be invested: gold coins, jewels, painting, stamps. It's not that big an undertaking. She fears the police here in America, so it is possible she will leave the country."

"Very possible. I believe she went to Tijuana, Mexico, but I don't think she'll stay there."

"Who would want to? It's a hell hole. But a good stopping off spot. She won't use her own passport, so a false one, or even better borrow one from someone who she resembles. Then south, out of Mexico, to a seaport. Then a ship to anywhere. Brazil, Argentina, Africa, Europe. Does she have good friends or relatives that she trusts?"

"Yes, in Sanrmeo, Italy."

Uncle brought his hands together in a loud clap. "A wonderful place to live out your remaining years. The casino is beautiful, and it is not as expensive as Rome, Paris, or the French Riviera."

Sanremo. Who else knew about her family there? Gaucho did, but what about Logan? I found Gaby's telephone bill and talked Mrs. Damonte into dialing the Sanremo number Gaby had called. I needed a little help from Mrs. D, and got much more than I could have hoped for.

"Don't mention Gaby directly. Her sister's first name is Ava. I'm not sure if she's married or even if she's alive. Try and find out who the number belongs to."

Mrs. D was reluctant at first, but once the connection was made she started babbling away as if she was chatting with her old cronies—chatting so fast that I couldn't keep up with the translation.

When she broke the connection, after close to ten minutes, she smiled at me. That didn't happen too often.

The number belonged to a restaurant, the Trattoria Di Vino, on Via Gaudio Street. The owner was Senora Ava Grinelli, whose maiden name was Maoret.

Mrs. D had spoken directly with the head waiter, Carmelo, who claimed that they served the best raviolis in town and that "*Les poissons sur l'assiette nageaient dans la mer ce matin-là.*"

The fish on the dinner plates were swimming in the sea that morning.

Ava Grinelli's husband has passed. One of her sons worked as the chef.

Mrs. D and Carmelo got along well, she telling him that she had spent a great deal of her youth in Sanremo.

Then she said that she thought Gaby was there, in Sanremo with her sister.

"Did the waiter tell you that?" I asked.

The answer was a hesitant no, but Carmelo did mention Ava was now living with her sister.

Then she asked if I was going to Italy to see Gaby.

"Yes. I'm afraid that she killed a man here in San Francisco."

Mrs. D rubbed a hand across her face.

"*L'uomo nella foto con il mastache?*"

The man in the picture with the mustache?

"Yes. Gaucho Carmichael. Seven years ago."

She squeezed her eyes shut, and then entwined her two index fingers. "*Sono insieme come uno.*"

They are together as one.

"Did she kill him?"

"*Solo gli spiriti lo sanno.*"

Only the spirits know. And apparently they weren't talking.

CHAPTER 16

The flight from San Francisco airport to Nice, France, was long—fourteen hours, with a stopover in Zurich, Switzerland.

The Nice Cote d'Azur airport is clean, nicely laid out, and, according to the on-plane brochures, the third busiest in all of France.

I hired a limo with driver, for the hour's drive to Sanremo, feeling like Banacek, the suave insurance investigator played by George Peppard in the 1970s' TV series.

The driver, Enrico, a scholarly looking man in his sixties, gave a running commentary as we cruised down the crescent-shaped strip of Mediterranean coastline with its rugged cliffs, clear blue water coves, picturesque seaside towns, fishing villages, stylish resort areas and emerald green golf courses.

My Italian was far from perfect, but we communicated well.

Sanremo has a population of fifty-seven thousand, according to Enrico. He gave me a quick tour, which included a visit to the Basilica Concattedrale di San Siro, with its twelve-bell church tower that Mrs. Damonte so envied.

Enrico dropped me off at the majestic Hotel Europa, which was just across the street from the casino and a three-minute walk to the beach.

I was tired from the trip so I napped, showered, and changed clothes. The local directories listed six Grinellis, none named Ava.

I took a tour of the casino, which looked like something out of a James Bond flick from the street.

The first floor wasn't much, you could have been in Reno; rows and rows of slot machines. The place to go is the second floor. You have to buy a daily membership, and there is a dress-code, no shorts or flip-flops, jackets for men. It's all lush carpeting, a mirrored ceiling, crystal chandlers with roulette, baccarat, blackjack and poker gaming tables manned by men in white shirts, bow ties, and black vests.

You half expect to see a tall, rugged-faced man in a tuxedo with a cigarette dangling from his mouth and a martini (shaken not stirred) in hand, bend over the baccarat table, drop a couple of thousand euros on the green felt and say "Banco."

I lost a few dollars and then headed for Trattoria Vino, a pleasant fifteen-block walk. Pleasant seemed to be the operative word for Sanremo. The weather was pleasant, as were the people, all polite smiles and nods.

Trattoria di Vino was a step up from pleasant; it was excellent, a small white-washed building tucked away on a quiet street away from the crowds.

There were just fourteen tables, all covered in rose-colored cloth that matched the waiter's jacket. The raviolis were as good as Mrs. D's (I wouldn't tell her that) and the fresh fish catch of the day was grilled cernia, a local grouper. All washed down with a bottle of Cinco Terre, a local white wine.

The waiter, Carmelo, was in his forties. The chef in the kitchen was of the same age, and a strapping young man in a muscle-bulging T-shirt did a little bit of everything.

There was no sign of a female employee.

When I was paying the bill, I asked Carmelo about Ava. "Someone told me to say hello to her."

He picked up my Yankee-tinted Italian accent right away.

"You are from America?"

"*Si*. New York."

"Ah, I wish to go there someday. Senora Ava only comes in on weekends now."

"She is in good health?"

He shook his hand back and forth. "*Mesa-mesa.* As good as can be expected."

Carmelo seemed to be getting a little suspicious, so I waved away the change, leaving him a healthy tip and exited the restaurant.

The next morning I did what any competent private investigator should do when he's staying at a high-class hotel in a strange town. I tipped Andres, the Hotel Europa's concierge, twenty American dollars and told him that I was interested in finding the home address of a woman named Ava Grinelli.

"She operates a nearby restaurant. Trattoria di Vino."

"Ah, a wonderful establishment. Do you wish me to make reservation?"

"No. I had dinner there last night. Apparently Ava is not in good health. I would like to stop and see her at her home."

Andres massaged the bill as if he expected the ink to rub off.

I added another twenty and told him that I was doing a

favor for a friend who knew Ava when she was very young. "He has a package for Ava, a surprise package. I want to deliver it to her personally."

Andres gave me a mock salute, then went behind his desk and began paging through phone books and making calls. Within ten minutes he came back with another smile and handed me a piece of hotel stationary. There was an address, and a hand drawn map.

"I believe you will find what you are looking for at this location, sir."

This location was a small, salmon-colored 1930s-style villa. I was to learn that there are no houses in Sanremo, only villas or apartments. The south wall was blanketed in flowering magenta-colored bougainvillea. There were plenty of fruit trees and planter boxes overflowing with roses.

A moss-green Alfa Romeo sedan was parked in the circular cobblestone driveway.

It was situated on a steep hill, just a few hundred yards from the Ligurian sea front.

I debated my next move. Knock on the door and ask for Gaby? Would she be there? Was Mrs. D losing her fortune telling skills? Was this all a wasted trip?

Not wasted, since the lovely Laura Feveral was waiting for me in Paris, only a scenic seven-hour train ride from Sanremo.

The decision turned out to be an easy one. At ten minutes past nine a tiny woman dressed in a denim jacket, faded jeans, a cowboy-style straw sunhat and sunglasses strolled out of the villa's front door. The jacket and hat were new, as was the golf putter in her right hand, stainless steel, not brass.

She walked with her head down, and it seemed that her pace was much slower now.

I slipped behind an oleander hedge as she passed by, and followed her down to a palm tree-edged promenade by the beach.

Joggers, runners, bicyclists strollers were taking full advantage of the warm, sunny weather.

She stopped and dug something out of her jacket pocket. For a second I thought that she's spotted me and was going to pull out her pearl handled pistol.

It turned out to be a pack of cigarettes and a lighter. She lit up, took several hard deep drags, and then continued on her walk.

When her pace picked up I called out, "Hi, Gaby."

She swiveled around, dropped the cigarette and cocked the golf putter behind her shoulder like a baseball player waiting for a fastball.

When she saw me she said, "Oh, shit!"

She kept the putter at the ready as she scanned the area.

"Where are the cops?"

"There are none, just me. Come on. Let's get some coffee."

She slipped off her sunglasses. Her eyes were red-rimmed and seemed lifeless. She led me to a small spot called, of all things, the Rolling Stone Café. There was outdoor seating with a view of the marina, where dozens of yachts were bobbing in the bay.

She ordered coffee and *Pescadores*, fisherman's cookies. We were silent until a young waitress in a checkered pink and white dress made the delivery, and then Gaby said, "How in the hell did you find me?"

"Some luck. I remembered the photo of you and your sister Ava, on the beach here. Then I checked your phone bill. One call, to the Trattorias de Vino last month. Why did you call the restaurant and not the house?"

"It was her birthday. I wanted to sing Happy Birthday to her. We always made our contacts by email. Just that once I called. Who else knows?"

"No one, yet."

There wasn't another customer within fifteen yards of us, but I leaned in close, lowered my voice and asked, "Why did you kill Gaucho?"

"I didn't kill him. I loved Gaucho."

She foraged in her jacket pockets for her cigarettes, taking out a pack of Lucky Strikes. I remembered her smoking when I'd first met her.

"I gave these damn things up again, for the hundred time, but then figured, what the hell. Enjoy what you can, while you can."

"Is IT really back?"

She used a Bic disposable lighter to get the cigarette going, exhaled a stream of smoke, appraised me though the haze, and when she spoke her voice was barely a whisper.

"Yep. I'm afraid IT is."

"Did you actually stop at a clinic in Tijuana?"

"For a couple of days. It felt like a scam, but there's a reputable cancer center here in Italy, the Sant'Orsola-Malpighi Hospital in Bologna, that I'm going to visit in a few days. Remember when I told you that God played a trick on us, Gaucho and me? Well, it was a dirty trick. I was getting better, but then he ends up with Big Casino, the biggest—pancreatic cancer. No cure. The timeline is four to eight months. Very painful months.

"So Gaucho wanted to get out. End it. Commit suicide. And he happened to have an expert on suicide in me. I had studied it, Nick. Researched all of the methods, because I was ready to check out myself. I came pretty close to doing it."

"So you assisted him?"

"I did."

"Seven years ago that was not legal in California, even if a physician was involved."

"Gaucho wanted it over quickly. And he didn't want anyone to know he'd done it. He kept talking about the trauma he went through when he found his father in the backyard in Texas."

"So how did he die?"

"Helium. An 'exit bag' they call it. A large plastic bag with a drawstring and a tube hooked up to a canister of helium. It's actually very simple. There's no pain, no gasping for breath. You're breathing in the helium rather than oxygen. It's the lack of oxygen that kills you."

"I remember seeing a box in the basement of the house on Greenwich Street, decorated with balloons. You told me it was helium."

"Yep. I kept one handy for myself."

"Someone told me that jumping off the Golden Gate Bridge was the best way to go."

"No. Some people have survived, and there's a chance the body will be recovered." She gave me a soft smile. "Besides, I'm afraid of heights. Believe me, I checked it out, I checked all of the options out: hanging, poisoning, drowning, cutting your wrists. No, helium is the way to go."

"How do I know you're telling me the truth? Inspector Larry Braun, remember him? He thinks you might have just gotten Gaucho drunk. There were two bottles of wine in the grave, and then shoved dirt over him."

"Inspector Braun? Is he after me?"

"Not personally. But the insurance investigator, Dan Forbes, is. He wants me to find you so that you can testify that Gaucho committed suicide."

She seemed genuinely puzzled. "Why?"

"Boston Fidelity wants to reclaim the insurance payout. And Logan and Paula Carmichael offered me fifteen thousand dollars to find you and have you to testify that he didn't kill himself."

"Is that why you're doing this, Nick. For the money?"

"I don't want the goddam money," I said louder than necessary, causing a few coffee drinkers to give me dirty looks.

"And don't you offer me any. What did you come away with? Over a million right, with the settlement from Logan and the Kelly painting."

"Gaucho gave me the painting."

"And you kept it in the safe in the wine cellar, didn't you?"

"That was his idea too. He knew that if his body was found right away, his brothers would go after me. Kick me out of the house, one way or another."

I pushed myself to my feet and took a short stroll, trying to clear my mind. When I got back to the table Gaby was tapping cigarette ash into her empty coffee cup.

"Give me the whole story," I told her. "Exactly how did Gaucho's suicide take place?"

"The hole was already in the ground, for the hot tub. We sat in lawn chairs, drank wine and listened to music, stuff he liked: tango, milonga, a kind of Argentine folk music, and some David Bowie. We drank, we cried, and then he said it was time."

Gaby wiped her eyes with a napkin before continuing.

"We put things in place. The bag, the tube, then turned on the helium. I held his hand the whole time. In about two minutes, he was unconscious. In ten, I knew he was dead. And, at Gaucho's request, I used the remaining helium to blow up some balloons, red, white and blue, and send them up into the night sky."

My coffee had gone cold, and I needed something stronger. The café had a full bar service so I signaled the waitress for some wine.

"Make it a bottle," Gaby suggested. "A chianti. I'm buying."

We didn't talk while the waitress went through the ritual of opening the bottle and pouring.

When she left I asked the question that was gnawing at my guts.

"So Gaucho passed. Then you just dumped him in the hole and covered him up?"

"Yes. It was all planned out very carefully, Nick. You have to remember that at the time, I was thinking I'd be taking a helium treatment soon myself. It was time to put my big girl's pants on. I covered him up, and put some outdoor furniture over the plot. The concrete came months later. We thought it would appear suspicious if the police saw a fresh slab of concrete."

"And then you drove his car down to Aquatic Park and left it there. With his clothes and Rolex."

"Again that was Gaucho's idea. He said to wait a week. His car was in the garage."

"It all seems so cold-blooded, Gaby."

"It was," she said, shaking her head from side to side. "But once you make up your mind to take your life, you turn cold. Ice cold."

She sipped her wine, and then said, "So now what? Are the cops coming here to arrest me? Are you taking me back to San Francisco?"

"Mrs. Damonte says that you and Gaucho are *Sono insieme come uno*. That your spirits are joined together."

"Lucinda. How is she? I miss her."

"She's fine, and she also says you cheat at cards. Gaby, I have no authority to do anything to you."

"But what if you tell the cops?"

"I don't think they'll be asking me about you."

"What about Gaucho's brothers? That bitch Paula? Or Forbes, the insurance guy? They offered you a lot of money to find me. What are you going to do?"

I couldn't see what good it would do to let the police know of Gaby's whereabouts. Prosecuting a seven-year-old assisted suicide case wasn't something that would interest them.

Boston Fidelity would be out the money, but they could afford it, and Gaucho would have passed, painfully, in a few months if he hadn't decided to end his own life, so they would have had to settle the claim. Logan Carmichael and Paula were coming out of it like the bandits they were. Maybe some of the money from the Greenwich Street house would go to making Niven Carmichael's life a little easier.

And Gaby. It wasn't my job to punish her. She'd gone through a lot of punishment already.

"I'm going to finish this glass of wine, check out of my hotel, and then take a trip to Paris and spend a week with a beautiful woman who I think I'm in love with. When I get back home, if anyone asks, I'll tell them the truth. Or at least part of it. That I learned you had checked into a Tijuana cancer clinic. And that you're dying as fast as you can. Let me know how you make out at the hospital in Bologna. Or, maybe you won't have to. Mrs. Damonte will find out from your spirits."

We clinked glasses and Gaby made a toast: "*Possiamo entrambi vivere fino a cento.*"

May we both live to be a hundred.

Who wouldn't drink to that?

ACKNOWLEDGMENTS

Thanks to Fred Hoedt for providing me with the title for this book.

JERRY KENNEALY has worked as a San Francisco policeman and as a licensed private investigator in the City by the Bay. He has written twenty-five novels, including a series on private eye Nick Polo, two of which were nominated for a Shamus Award. His books have been published in England, France, Germany, Japan, Italy, and Spain. He is a member of Mystery Writers of America and Private Eye Writers of America.

He was the recipient of the 2017 Life Achievement Award by the Private Eye Writers of America.

Jerry lives in San Bruno, California, with his wife and in-house editor, Shirley.

https://www.facebook.com/jerry.kennealy

On the following pages are a few more great titles from the Down & Out Books publishing family.

For a complete list of books and to sign up for our newsletter, go to DownAndOutBooks.com.

I Know Where You Sleep
A P.I. Thriller
Alan Orloff

Down & Out Books
February 2020
978-1-64396-077-7

A relentless stalker has been terrorizing Jessica Smith, and, out of good options, she finally turns to her last resort—PI Anderson West.

With some overzealous help from his loose-cannon sister Carrie, West unearths a horde of suspicious men in Jessica's life. But are any twisted enough to terrorize her?

When Jessica disappears, it's up to West to find her before the stalker does.

Pushing Water
A Penns River Crime Novel
Dana King

Down & Out Books
May 2020
978-1-64396-073-9

An active shooter at a local discount department store in Penns River leaves several people dead and the shooter in the wind. Maybe. It's hard to say as the man arrested at the scene definitely shot someone but claims to be a Good Guy with a Gun.

Meanwhile, a Canadian fugitive lands in town and pulls a job to tide him over while his cache of cash makes its way across the border. He and his partner—a local just dumb enough to serve a purpose—see an opportunity and begin a robbery spree while the police focus on clearing the mass shooting.

this letter to Norman Court
Part One of the Trevor English Series
Pablo D'Stair

All Due Respect, an imprint of
Down & Out Books
January 2020
978-1-64396-095-1

When petty crook Trevor English is offered two thousand dollars to deliver a letter across the country, the choice seems fairly simple—money up front, no way he can go wrong.

And when he finds himself in possession of correspondence several parties would pay to get their hands on, the choice seems even simpler—take what he can, while he can, from who he can…and disappear.

Chasing China White
Allan Leverone

Shotgun Honey, an imprint of
Down & Out Books
September 2019
978-1-64396-029-6

When heroin junkie Derek Weaver runs up an insurmountable debt with his dealer, he's forced to commit a home invasion to wipe the slate clean.

Things go sideways and Derek soon finds himself a multiple murderer in the middle of a hostage situation.

With seemingly no way out, he may discover the key to redemption lies in facing down long-ignored demons.

Made in the USA
Columbia, SC
06 March 2021

33463676R00098